SUSPICION

SUSPICION

A PRIVATE NOVEL

KATE BRIAN

SIMON AND SCHUSTER

First published in Great Britain in 2010 by Simon and Schuster UK Ltd
A CBS COMPANY

Originally published in the USA in 2009 by Simon Pulse,
an imprint of Simon & Schuster Children's Division, New York.

 Produced by Alloy Entertainment
151 West 26th Street, New York, NY 10001

Simon & Schuster UK Ltd
1st Floor, 222 Gray's Inn Road, London WC1X 8HB

This book is a work of fiction. Names, characters, places and incidents are either
the product of the author's imagination or are used fictitiously. Any resemblance
to actual people living or dead, events or locales is entirely coincidental.

A CIP catalogue record for this book is available from the British Library.

ISBN 978-1-8473879-4

1 3 5 7 9 10 8 6 4 2

Printed and bound in Great Britain.

www.simonandschuster.co.uk

For Brady

SUSPICION

SURVIVAL

The important thing is not to panic.

Like that was even possible. My heart pounded erratically in my chest, radiating terror through my veins. I had been treading water in the dark of night for maybe ten minutes, but it might as well have been ten hours. The floaty chiffon gown that had seemed so light and airy when I had selected it for the Ryans' Casino Night now clung to my skin and tangled around my legs, threatening to pull me down. Down into the deep, dark depths of the ocean where who-knew-what disgusting, slimy, razor-toothed thi ngs were waiting to nibble on my toes and fingers and—

No.

No. No. No. It was going to be okay. It was, it was, it was. If I could just keep my eye on the Ryans' boat, everything would be fine. I could still hear the piano music drifting across the Caribbean Sea, could still make out the cheers as a guest won big at the card tables. As long as I could see the boat there was the possibility it might come back for me. I stared at the merrily twinkling lights on the deck as the vessel sailed back toward St. Barths and willed it to turn. Sent a silent panic signal to anyone who might care. Noelle. Upton. Kiran. Dash. Taylor. Tiffany. *Someone please just realize I'm not there. Someone go looking for me. Someone, anyone, hear me.*

I caught a stray shout and my heart leapt with hope. But the shout was followed by a peal of laughter. They were just obliviously going about their partying. Everyone I knew on the island was on that boat. And it was quickly floating out of reach.

The important thing is not to panic.

But the mantra wasn't working. Someone on that boat had tried to kill me. Someone had torn off the ridiculously expensive diamond necklace I'd been wearing—Noelle's necklace—and shoved me overboard into the frigid water. A slim, hooded figure. Average height. That was all I had seen after plunging into the sea and struggling to the surface. A hooded figure slinking away, the white trim on the black hood practically glowing in the moonlight. I couldn't tell if it was male or female, old or young, but I had my suspicions. Poppy Simon, Paige Ryan, or Sienna Marquez. They were all jealous of me. They all wanted Upton Giles, my new sort-of boyfriend. One of them clearly wanted him enough to murder me and get me out of the way.

And it looked like she was going to succeed.

No.

I was not going to let her win. Whichever one of those psychos had done this was going to be sorely disappointed. I couldn't wait until she saw me alive. I was going to walk up to her and spit in her face. And right after I did that, I was getting the hell off of St. Barths. This place was pure evil. I would have been better off vacationing on the time-hopping torture island from *Lost*.

The skirt of my dress wrapped around my right ankle and held fast, restricting my movement. Without a second thought I reached for the zipper at the side of the gown and, my cold fingers trembling and slipping, managed to yank it down. After a brief struggle I was free of the thing. It floated off on the waves like a lazy sapphire-blue cloud bobbing in the wind. Instantly, I felt twenty pounds lighter, and proud of myself for having made such a wise decision. I took a deep breath and realized that I was moving my arms much faster than I needed to, so I forced myself to slow down. Soon my heart rate calmed and my breathing stabilized. This was much better. I was strong. I was an athlete. I could tread water like this for hours.

Maybe. How long *could* a person tread water, technically? I had no idea. It wasn't a fact I'd ever thought I would need to know, hailing as I did from a landlocked state. But here I was, little Reed Brennan of Croton, Pennsylvania, treading for her life, half naked in the Caribbean Sea.

How the hell had I gotten here?

"I picked the wrong guy," I answered aloud. "Again."

My voice sounded odd and unbearably lonely. I resolved not to talk anymore. But now that I'd started thinking of Upton, I couldn't stop. If only I had stuck to my original instinct and steered clear of him, none of this would be happening. But how could I have resisted a gorgeous, incredible, worldly British guy coming at me full force with all his talk of how different and amazing I was? I was only human. And yeah, maybe he had been with a lot of girls, but how was I supposed to know that one of them was going to turn out to be homicidal?

Come on, Reed. Try learning from experience.

I looked at the boat and my entire body jolted with terror. The lights were winking in and out on the horizon. Winking. Winking. Winking. And then they were gone.

I whirled around with a splash, searching the endless waterscape. There had to be another boat. A light. A buoy. Anything. But all I could see for miles was the deep blue of the ocean, lit by the thousands of stars overhead. No land, no vessels, nothing. Nothing but water. I was alone. Alone and adrift in the middle of nowhere.

No one was coming for me. I was going to drown out here. By myself. In the dark. They would never even find my body. I was going to drift out here forever at the bottom of the ocean.

No. Stop. Just stop.

I couldn't let myself go there. Couldn't think that way. No matter how true it felt in that moment, I could not start thinking the worst. I had survived so much. I could survive this. I just had to give my tired limbs a break. I took a deep breath and forced myself to lie back and float, even though it meant taking my eyes off the horizon. I would float for a few minutes, regain my strength, and then start treading again. It was going to be okay. It was all going to be okay.

The stars formed a close-knit blanket across the sky. I had never seen so many in my life. It was beautiful. If it was the last thing I saw, it wouldn't be so bad. I wondered what it would be like to drown. Whether it would hurt. I thought of Thomas Pearson and the awful manner in which he had died, murdered by a girl who claimed to love him. A crazy girl with a baseball bat. I wished he were here with me now. If I only had the chance, I would tell him how sorry I was. I would tell him that I hoped Ariana Osgood had done the deed quickly. That he didn't have too much time to be scared. Like me. I was going to have a lot of time to be scared . . . terrified . . . desperate . . . before I finally went.

My heart seized in panic as the reality of the situation slammed into my chest, and for a brief moment, I went under. Salty water filled my mouth and nostrils, and my lungs exploded with pain. I fought my way to the surface again, flailing and gasping for air. There was still nothing. Nothing but the ocean and the sky. Midnight blue as far as the eye could see. Stars everywhere, but nothing else. Nothing but the ripples atop the water. I was never going to be able to survive this. Never, never, never.

But somehow, I kept treading. Minutes passed. Hours. I had no idea how long I had been out there when my limbs started to feel impossibly heavy. When my mind started to grow so very tired. I tried to float again, and as I lay back my eyes fluttered closed. Instantly I saw a flash of Sabine DuLac, her face twisted with ire, and I felt her hands grab my shoulders and shove me down. I struggled against her, but the more I squirmed and writhed, the further I sank. She was pushing, pushing, pushing me down. I opened my eyes under the water and they stung from the salt. I could see nothing. Nothing but . . . a shadow. Something moving. Something dark. And it wasn't very far away.

My heart burst with fear. I clawed my way to the surface and heaved in a breath, flailing around in the ocean, trying to find whatever it was I had seen under the water. Was it a shark, or a harmless fish? A turtle? A dolphin? A whale? I had no idea how big or small it was. How far away or how near.

Suddenly I felt something slither around my ankle. I screamed and kicked and started to cry. *My God, please don't let anything be down there. Please just let it be my paranoia taking over.*

But there it was again. Something sliding across my toes. I screamed again and swam a few feet away, my tired muscles barely functioning. As if a few strokes were going to free me from a water dweller. If something out here wanted me as its midnight snack, it was pretty much going to have me.

I was sobbing now. Gulping for air. Afraid that at any second I would feel it again. Or worse, that I would feel jaws close around my foot. See a fin sailing ominously by. I gasped in a breath and started to choke. Water filled my mouth and throat and I spit it out, coughing, choking, struggling for air.

I had to get a grip. If I didn't, my panic attack was going to drown me.

Maybe it was nothing. Maybe I was just imagining things. Or maybe it was seaweed. Or even my dress. Maybe it was still nearby but had sunk below the surface.

I took a breath. Yes. That was it. I told myself it was just the dress.

And even though I didn't completely believe it, my breathing started to return to normal.

But still, the tears came. And suddenly, I was thinking about Josh Hollis. Josh, who was back in the States, probably out to dinner or cuddling on the couch somewhere with his girlfriend, Ivy Slade. I imagined what he would do when he heard of my death. Would he cry? Scream? Throw a fit of despair? He'd already lost his best friend. Would losing me push him over the edge? Or was he falling in love with Ivy? Had he already forgotten me? Would the news of my death be just one more tragedy, a story they could tell their kids as they grew older, how daddy's old girlfriend drowned tragically off the coast of St. Barths?

I scoffed a laugh at the thought of Josh and Ivy as a married couple. Forget Josh. What would Upton do? Would he miss me? Or would he just move on to the next girl? Would he ever know that it was one of his deranged exes who had done this? Would he even care?

The guy had claimed he loved me. But if he was so in love with me, how could he have just left me in the Ryans' stateroom like that? We had gone down there to snag a little alone time and been caught half undressed by Mrs. Ryan and Poppy, one of Upton's many ex-hookups. But instead of staying with me and pep talking me out of my abject humiliation, he had gone after Poppy to make sure she was okay. Was he still with her right now? Had he even realized I was missing? Why hadn't he come to save me?

My chin dipped under the water and I surged up again. My arms were moving slower and slower. My eyes had closed. I was falling asleep. For a moment I fought against it, but I felt my lids growing heavy again. And then my nose was under. Heart panicking, I pushed up with all my might, but I barely got my chin above the surface.

This was it. I had nothing left. I had done my best, but this was how I was going to die. I thought of my mother. Of how sad she would be. And my dad. He definitely wasn't going to take this well. I hoped my brother, Scott, would be there for them. The thought of the three of them alone together, without me, brought tears to my eyes and made my nose clog. *I'm so sorry . . . but I can't do this anymore. . . .*

"There! I see something! Right over there! Shine the light!"

I closed my eyes. I was hallucinating. It was really over.

And slowly, I started to sink into the inky blue depths of the sea.

"Reed! Over here! I'm coming!"

I blinked. My brain told me I was hallucinating, but I raised my right hand just in case. The effort did me in, and instantly, I sank like a stone. Just before the water closed over my face, just before my eyes fluttered closed for the last time, I caught the briefest glimpse of a blond-haired boy tearing off his shirt and diving into the water.

DRAMATIC TEENAGERS

Through the slats of the white vinyl blinds, I could see palm trees. They rustled in the wind, backdropped by an impossibly blue sky. Big puffy white clouds chased one another across the window and out of view. Somewhere nearby a bird chirped happily. Where the hell was I? Why was the window on the wrong side of the bed? What was that incessant beeping and why wouldn't it stop?

The brightness of the sun was too much. I turned my head away from the window and felt a tug on my neck, like something was stuck to the skin there. I reached my hand up to inspect and froze. Sitting at the end of my bed—a hospital bed, I now realized with a jolt—was Sawyer Hathaway, his hands clasped together under his chin. He was wearing a tuxedo shirt open over his bare chest, along with a pair of blue scrubs. His light blond hair was a tousled mess, as if it had air dried hours ago and not seen a comb since.

"Sawyer?" I croaked.

His gray eyes popped open and relief flooded his face. "You're awake." He stood up and moved so close to the head of the bed that I could see the flecks of brown in his irises. "Are you okay?"

As if that was even worth discussing. I simply stared up at him. "You saved my life."

A blush lit his chiseled cheeks. He gripped the metal guardrail at the side of my bed, his knuckles white. "How do you feel?"

"What's this thing on my neck?" I asked, lifting my hand.

I winced in pain and my arm dropped back down again. My muscles felt like lifeless bags of flour, as if I'd spent an entire day in the weight room at Easton. I tried to move my legs. Same thing.

"I can't move," I whimpered, closing my eyes.

"You were treading water for three hours," Sawyer said.

"Three hours?" My eyes popped open again. "How did you even find me?"

Sawyer pulled his chair from the foot of the bed and sat right next to me. He clasped his hands and rested his elbows on his thighs, leaning forward.

"When Upton couldn't find you at the party he got worried and sent everyone out to search the boat," he explained. His voice sounded pinched. Like he was fighting for control. "No one could find you anywhere and Noelle lost it. Her dad insisted that the police send out search boats, and we all grabbed whatever boats we could find and searched too." He unclasped his hands and rubbed them over his knees. "I was in a boat with Noelle and my dad and brother, so it's not like it was just me who saved you."

"Please," I said, my heart welling as I remembered the fear, the sadness, the resignation. "I was just about to give up. If it wasn't for you . . ." I took a deep, broken breath. "Thank you, Sawyer."

His face lit up. For a moment it looked like he was trying to squash it, but the smile won out. Sawyer Hathaway looked me in the eye and smiled. It was only the second time I'd seen him do that since I'd arrived on the island. It was a very nice smile.

"You're welcome," he said simply.

"What time is it?" I asked. "Actually . . . what day is it?"

Sawyer smirked. "It's December twenty-seventh. And it's a little after three. You've been sleeping all day."

I took a deep breath. I felt like I could sleep for *ten* days.

A hefty nurse with dark skin and long black hair stepped into the room, wearing a starchy-looking pink uniform. She widened her eyes at us, then angled her head back into the hallway.

"She's awake!"

When she walked back into the room, she was followed by two police officers, one of them black, the other white. They were both tall, the black man broad and muscular, while his counterpart was more wiry. Both had stern, no-nonsense looks on their faces that made me instantly feel as if I was in trouble. They wore light blue polo shirts with blue shorts that showed their knees and leg hair, and sort of undermined their authority. I glanced at Sawyer, who had sat up straight at their entrance. His gaze was fixed on the cops.

"Good afternoon, Miss Brennan!" the nurse said in a Caribbean accent, walking around to the far side of my bed, across from Sawyer. "We are very happy to see you up and awake!"

"Thank you," I replied, keeping one eye on the cops while she wrapped a blood pressure gauge around my upper arm. I realized for the first time that I was wearing a thin hospital gown, underpants, and nothing else. No bra to speak of. Then I realized with a start that when Sawyer had saved me I had been floating in the water in nothing but a tiny pair of black undies and an even skimpier strapless bra. My face burned, wondering how much, exactly, he, Graham, and Mr. Hathaway had seen.

"Miss Brennan, I'm Officer Marshall; this is Officer Gravois," the white policeman said, pulling a small notebook out of the pocket of his shirt as he nodded at his partner. "How are you feeling?"

"Okay. Tired," I replied.

He smiled slightly, but his partner maintained his dire expression.

"That's understandable. But when you feel up to it, we'd like to ask you a few questions about your accident," Officer Marshall said.

Accident? I felt an instant flash of shock and anger. The nurse removed the blood pressure gauge with a loud rip and I struggled to push myself up onto my elbows. The pain in my muscles was excruciating, but I managed to get there. Again, the bandage on my neck pulled at my skin, and I placed my hand over it, trying to calm a burning sensation beneath the dressing.

"I can talk about it now, thanks, and it wasn't an accident," I said. "I was pushed."

"What?" Sawyer blurted.

"Pushed?" the nurse echoed.

"Excuse me?" Officer Gravois asked dubiously, speaking for the first time. He had a French-Caribbean accent, like the nurse did, which somehow made him sound even more condescending than he looked.

"Someone on the boat tried to kill me," I said firmly. "They tore off my necklace and shoved me overboard."

I winced, remembering the priceless jewels Noelle had lent me. Jewels that were now lost forever. That explained the burning sensation on my neck. The bandage must have been covering a cut left by all those diamonds and sapphires.

"Someone shoved you," Officer Marshall said flatly.

Their doubt shot under my skin and I pushed myself up higher. The nurse procured some pillows from a closet at the foot of the bed and pushed them behind me, helping me to sit up.

"All I remember is this musky smell . . . like cologne or perfume," I said. "And then someone ripped off my necklace and pushed me. That's how I got this cut." I turned my head so they could see the bandage. "Whoever did this is a thief and a murderer."

"That would be *attempted* murderer," Officer Gravois corrected with a chuckle. His partner hid a smile behind his hand. I noticed he was holding a pencil, but had yet to write down anything in his trusty notebook.

"You don't believe me?" I demanded.

"Perhaps you are confused," Officer Gravois said. "Or perhaps you feel embarrassed because the entire St. Barths police force was sent out looking for you for hours. You want to make it seem as if you are a victim, not a mere . . . what is the word . . . klutz?"

Okay. *Now* I was pissed.

"I'm not a klutz! Someone wants me dead. How can you not believe me?"

"You were drinking, no?" Officer Gravois said.

Suddenly I felt even more alone than I had out in the open ocean. I needed help. Someone was trying to *kill* me and these were the people who were supposed to help. It was their job. But apparently they were too lazy to *do* their job and preferred instead to mock me. Desperation burbled up in my veins, making my heart race like I'd downed ten cups of espresso.

"Actually, *no*," I spat. "I had one glass of champagne. If I were drunk enough to imagine this entire thing, do you really think I could have treaded water for that long?"

"It wasn't *that* long," Officer Marshall said, flipping the pages in his notebook to check it. "It was only about three and a half hours."

"That's a long time!" Sawyer and I said in unison.

I glanced at Sawyer, grateful that I had someone on my side. The cops looked at each other, clearly amused by our overly dramatic antics.

"Look, you don't understand. This isn't the first time," I said, growing more frustrated. "First, someone spooked my horse and almost sent me headlong over a cliff. Then my Jet Ski went haywire and exploded, and now this. Someone on the island is after me."

My heart pounded as I told the story. I realized with a start that whoever was after me would probably try again. No. Not probably. Definitely. They'd already tried three times, so clearly, they were determined to get the job done. I swallowed hard, trying to dampen my fear.

"Miss Brennan, you must calm down," the nurse said, touching her fingertips to my arm. "You need your rest."

"I'll rest if you tell these guys to listen to me," I blurted. "What's going on here?"

Mr. Lange's booming voice filled the room as he stormed in, followed by Noelle and Upton. I had never seen a more welcome sight in my life. Not only did the jackass police look instantly intimidated by Noelle's father, but Noelle and Upton's mere presence made me feel safe.

"We're just interviewing Miss Brennan, sir," one of the officers said. But I wasn't paying attention, because I was too busy staring at Upton and wishing I could touch him. Suddenly, more than anything, I just needed to cuddle into his arms and stay there for about ten years. But the room was so full now, he couldn't even get close enough to me to touch my hand. He and Noelle hung back near the foot of the bed while the nurse changed my IV bag. Noelle looked at me like she just wanted to hug me. I knew the feeling.

"Harassing her is what it sounded like," Mr. Lange replied, crossing his arms over his chest. His handsome face was red with anger, the little lines around his mouth deeper than usual as he frowned. He glanced over at Sawyer and me. "What's going on?"

"Reed told them she was pushed off the boat and they don't believe her," Sawyer said matter-of-factly.

"Pushed?" Noelle asked. She walked over to me now, practically shoving the nurse aside. Her long brown hair tumbled down her back in unwashed waves and she wore a plain white T-shirt, black shorts, and zero makeup. The most basic outfit I'd ever seen on her. "Who pushed you?"

"I don't know," I replied, my voice sounding small. "But I saw a . . . someone in a hooded jacket," I said, suddenly recalling. I glared at the officers. "I saw them moving away from the railing when I broke the surface."

"Can you describe this person?" Officer Marshall asked, his pencil at the ready. He cast a sidelong glance at Mr. Lange, as if he wanted to make sure Noelle's dad saw him doing his job.

"No," I said. "I couldn't make out their face from the water."

The nurse slunk out behind the officers' backs.

"You have to admit, it sounds a bit far-fetched," Officer Marshall said, looking at Noelle's father.

Mr. Lange took a step closer to the officers. "If the girl says she was pushed, she was pushed. I expect you to take her accusation seriously."

The two officers glanced at each other over Mr. Lange's shoulder. I could tell they were still doubtful, but they finally acquiesced.

"Yes, sir. Of course," Officer Marshall said. "Of course there will be a full investigation."

"Good," Mr. Lange said. "I'll be calling your supervisor to make sure your department is aware of the gravity of the situation."

Officer Gravois's jaw clenched. I could tell he did not like the sound of this, and I was glad. Glad that he was unhappy. He looked over at me and attempted a smile. "Get some rest, Miss Brennan. We're glad you're all right."

Yeah. Sure you are. More like you're pissed off that I just created actual work for you to do.

The two cops left the room and we could hear them bitching to each other in French all the way down the hall. Mr. Lange whipped out his cell phone and speed dialed someone, his lips set in a tight line.

"I'm going to go speak to the doctors," he said, holding the phone away from his ear for a moment. "Someone should be in here checking you out right now." As he walked out he barked into the phone. "Get me the St. Barths police department. Now."

"Thanks," I called after him meekly. Finally, Noelle, Upton, Sawyer, and I were alone.

"That's Daddy. Always multitasking," Noelle joked.

"He doesn't have to do all this," I said, a bit awed by his concern for and defense of me.

"Sure he does. He likes to be in control," Noelle said with a shrug.

Like father, like daughter. I heard him pause to talk to some people out in the hallway and recognized Taylor Bell's voice. I glanced at Noelle quizzically.

"A bunch of people came to make sure you were okay," she explained. "Dash, Kiran, Taylor, Tiff, Amberly, Gage, West . . ."

All my friends from Easton. Even Gage Coolidge, who usually called me Farm Girl. And Amberly, who was closer to frenemy than friend. Of course Poppy, Paige, Sienna, and Daniel, Paige's brother, hadn't shown. Why was I not surprised?

"You guys believe me, right?" I asked, looking around at my friends.

"Of course," Sawyer replied.

My heart welled with gratitude. I was about to thank him, but then Upton walked over and paused next to his chair. "You mind, mate?" he said.

Sawyer glanced at him, hesitated, then got up, pushing the chair toward the wall with the back of his legs without a word. Upton leaned over and kissed my lips, running his hand over my forehead before dropping right down in Sawyer's vacated seat.

"Just calm down and get some rest," he said, clasping my hand in both of his. His deep voice and sexy English accent sent a pleasant thrill down my spine. The first pleasant sensation I'd had since I woke up. "We can deal with all of this later. Right now you just have to take care of yourself."

"Okay," I said, my voice full. "I'm so glad you guys are here," I added, glancing at Noelle.

"We're not going anywhere," Noelle replied, pulling up another chair from under the window. "Just try to get some sleep."

I nodded and leaned back into the pillows, clinging to Upton's hand. A sense of peace came over me and I felt my eyelids growing heavy. Everything was going to be okay. Upton and Noelle would take care of me. And Sawyer. Sawyer had saved me. I wouldn't even be here if not for him. Plus, he believed me. He was the only one other than Mr. Lange who had actually said he believed me.

I forced my tired eyes open, intending to thank him again, but when I glanced around the room, he was already gone.

STAY

My bags were packed and placed next to the front door of the Langes' house, along with the footlocker brimming with college sweatshirts that Upton had given me for Christmas. Mr. Lange barked into his cell phone at the police, pacing around the glass topped coffee table in the great room of the Langes' vacation home. I stood near the door, my fingers toying with the tiny shell on my rope necklace a Christmas gift from Sawyer, which I had put on for the first time that morning. I stared at the footlocker, letting my eyes focus and blur, focus and blur.

I'd been so happy on Christmas Eve. So in the moment with Upton. I wished we could have just stayed there forever, hanging out on the floor of his father's study. Alone together. Where no one could touch us. I had to get out of here. How could I stay after everything that had happened? But I felt the loss of everything this trip could have been. It pressed against my chest like an iron fist.

"Is that everything?" Noelle asked, coming up behind me.

I jumped and let out an involuntary yelp. Apparently almost getting killed three times in a week can make a girl jumpy.

"Sorry. I forgot. No sneak attacks," Noelle said, touching my shoulder lightly.

Her hair was back in a loose bun and she wore a black T-shirt dress with a neckline so wide the right side fell off her shoulder, exposing her perfectly tanned skin. She looked like a girl without a care in the world. Someone ready to spend her day lazing on the beach sipping piña coladas, just waiting for some hot guy to come along and reapply her suntan lotion. I had never been more envious of her than I was in that moment.

Carefree was not a state with which I was familiar.

"Yeah. That's everything," I said.

"Are you sure about this?" Noelle asked. "If you stay I swear I won't let you out of my sight for the rest of the trip."

"That's comforting, but no thanks," I said, taking a deep breath. "My parents are expecting me today and my mother is kind of freaking out after everything that's happened. I think she'll lose it if she doesn't actually get to see me and make sure I'm in one piece."

Noelle smirked. "Parents."

"I know. Besides, whoever's after me is on this island, so I think the best thing to do is just to get the hell off of it," I added.

"Get the hell off of what?"

"Omigod," I breathed, my hand flying to my chest.

Upton had walked up behind us from the great room, once again scaring the wind right out of me. He was wearing a soft-looking navy blue polo and white linen pants, and his feet were bare. His light brown hair had been tousled by the ocean breeze and he made no move to fix it. He was gorgeous. Of course he was. But my heart didn't skip in excitement upon seeing him, like it had every other time he'd entered a room. Since being released from the hospital the afternoon before, I had been trying not to think about all those hours in the water alone. Instead, I'd been focusing on what had happened before my ignominious plunge.

Namely, that Upton had left me alone at one of the most humiliating moments of my life and run off to comfort Poppy Simon, the girl he had been hooking up with for the past few months—until he met me. Poppy was the person he'd been worried about after she and Mrs. Ryan had caught the two of us rolling around on the bed in Mrs. Ryan's stateroom. Her feelings were the ones that mattered to him. Not mine. When I'd seen him at the hospital, my mind hadn't even gone there. I was so happy just to be with him again, to be alive, that I'd momentarily spaced on how much he'd hurt me.

But now I remembered. And I was not happy.

"Where did you come from?" Noelle asked. She shot him a narrow-eyed look. I had told Noelle the entire stateroom story the night before, and she had been about ready to drive over to Upton's and wring his neck. Girl always had my back.

"Walked up from the beach," Upton replied, tilting his head toward the sliding glass doors that fronted the white sand and the pristine turquoise ocean beyond. His sandy flip-flops had been left by the open door. "I was going to ring you, but it's such a gorgeous day I decided on a stroll instead. Now who's getting the hell off what?"

"I am," I said tonelessly. I picked up my hoodie, which I'd flung over the top of my suitcase, and shoved my arms into it. "I'm getting the hell off this island."

Upton's eyebrows shot up in surprise. "What? Why?"

He sounded shocked. Like he couldn't think of a single reason I might want to go. I felt so angry and defensive that my shoulders actually curled.

"You seriously need to ask?" I blurted, zipping the sweatshirt violently. "In case you've come down with a case of sudden amnesia, one of your jilted girlfriends is trying to *kill* me. I'm not going to stick around here and give her the opportunity to finish the job."

Noelle and Upton exchanged a look that made me want to grab the back of their heads and knock their skulls together. In the great room, Mr. Lange lowered his voice and paced over to the doors, staring out at the ocean as he spoke.

"Are you *laughing* at me?" I demanded, my face growing hot.

"It's just . . . we know these people, Reed. We've known them since we were zygotes," Noelle said. "They're not capable of murder."

"Yeah, but two years ago you never would've thought Ariana could kill anyone either," I shot back, staring her down.

Noelle's jaw clenched, but she never broke eye contact. She'd never been one to back down from a direct challenge, even when she was 100 percent wrong.

"For the record, I would have," Upton said, raising a hand. "Girl was always a bit dodgy in my opinion."

"Shut up, Upton," Noelle said impatiently. "Okay, I never would've thought Ariana could kill anyone either, but Ariana was different. Poppy and Paige . . . they don't have the guts to do something like this."

"What about Sienna? You haven't known *her* since you were 'zygotes,'" I said sarcastically, throwing in some air quotes.

"No, but Sienna is harmless," Upton said, stepping closer to me.

"Harmless? She left me in a shower stall for hours, freezing my ass off with no clothes," I replied.

"Right. I'd forgotten about that," Upton said, looking at his feet. "Okay, so she's not harmless, but she's not a violent person. You have to be quite mad to commit murder, Reed, and that's not Sienna."

His tone was placating, almost condescending. I glanced at Noelle. Both of them were looking at me as if I was some irrationally scared toddler. Like I'd just woken up from a nightmare and they were trying to convince me that the monsters weren't real. But they *were* real. Someone had pushed me off that boat. I had felt their hands, smelled their fragrance, *seen* them slink away. Why didn't anyone want to believe me?

"I don't understand how you guys can act like nothing's wrong," I said, desperation welling inside my chest, constricting my lungs. "Someone is trying to kill me. They spooked my horse, they rigged my Jet Ski, they shoved me off a moving boat. Three times in the last week I've almost *died*. Don't you get it? I can't stay here."

Tears welled up in my eyes, which frustrated me even more; I was playing into their image of me as a frightened, irrational baby. I took a deep breath and forced myself to calm down. My vision was blurry as I glared at them in defiance, but no tears escaped.

"Reed, Misty and the Jet Ski . . . those were simply accidents," Upton said, taking my hands lightly in his.

I clucked my tongue. "No, they—"

"But if you say someone pushed you off the boat, then someone pushed you off the boat," Upton added, interrupting me. "And if you stay here, you'll be available to the police. Maybe you'll remember something that will help them sort it all out."

I scoffed, my voice bubbly and wet. "Please. They're not even going to investigate this. They think I'm some drunk, spoiled liar."

"Oh, they're investigating it," Noelle said, glancing over her shoulder at her father, whose back was to us. "You saw how pissed off Daddy was. Believe me, he's going to take care of it."

Mr. Lange's phone snapped shut and he huffed a sigh, muttering under his breath as he approached us. As always, his clothes were crisp and pressed—a light yellow button-down shirt over gray pants—but he looked tired. Exhausted, actually. He pressed the top of his nose between his thumb and forefinger before addressing me.

"Reed, I'm so sorry, but it looks like we won't have access to the jet until tomorrow," he said.

"What? Why?" Noelle asked.

His nostrils flared slightly. "Your mother has seen fit to fly it back to the States to pick up some sort of flowers she simply *must* have for the centerpieces at the gala," he replied sarcastically.

Noelle sighed. "That's Mom for you."

Noelle's mother was hosting her annual hospital benefit on the island the following week. She had been wrapped up in the plans ever since we'd arrived, and I'd barely laid eyes on her, even though I'd been living in her house for the past week. Which made sense if she was jaunting around the island in search of flowers.

"There is one commercial flight leaving for Philadelphia later today," Mr. Lange said, checking the screen of his phone. "You'd have to connect through Atlanta, and of course I'd hire a car to drive you the rest of the way to Croton once you arrived. I feel horrible about this."

"See? Now you *must* stay," Upton said, squeezing my hand.

I loved how flying commercial wasn't even an option for him. Before last year I'd never been on any kind of plane, never mind been spoiled into thinking a private jet was the only civilized way to go.

"No. It's okay. I'll take the commercial flight," I replied, pulling my fingers away. Upton, for the first time, seemed to sense the cold vibe I was giving off. His brow creased and he pushed his hands into his pockets, looking dejected.

"Are you sure?" Mr. Lange asked. "I can have the jet gassed and ready for you first thing in the morning."

"Yes, I'm sure," I replied. "I'll go today."

"I'll call my travel agent." Mr. Lange flipped open the phone again, but Noelle held up a hand.

"Wait, Daddy."

He did. She turned to face me.

"Reed, come on. Just sit tight one more day," she said. "We can stay here on our beach, hang out at the house. I promise you won't have to see Poppy, Paige, or Sienna if you don't want to. You should get at least one day of relaxation out of this trip."

I looked into her eyes and realized with a start that she felt guilty. Like all of this was somehow her fault. Why? Because she was the one who had invited me here? That was crazy. She had been trying to do something nice for me. It wasn't her fault one of her friends had turned out to be a sociopath.

"Besides, you heard what Mr. Lange said," Upton added. "You can take the private jet in the morning. You'll be so much more comfortable and it'll take half the time."

Apparently my coldness hadn't completely shut him down. Which was kind of nice. Part of me was glad that he wasn't simply giving up on me. But if I stayed, I was going to have to talk to him. Figure out what had happened, what it meant, and where we stood. The very thought exhausted me.

"Please?" Noelle asked.

That one word stopped me cold. Noelle almost never said "please." To her, just saying the word was akin to begging, which was *not* her style. I felt my resolve start to cave. I glanced at Upton, whose blue eyes stared back at me, open, questioning, almost vulnerable.

"Okay, fine," I said finally, feeling my resolve melt. "But first thing in the morning, I am on that plane."

NONTRAGIC

I took a deep breath, filling my lungs with warm, tropical air, and held it as I looked up at the blue-and-white brocade pattern of the umbrella overhead. The breeze fluttered the trim and blew the pages of Noelle's magazine over her hand. Digging my toes into the toasty sand, I let out the breath and felt relaxed for the first time all day.

"Okay, maybe you were right," I said, lifting my head from the soft beach blanket. "Maybe staying another day was a good idea."

My parents hadn't been too psyched when I'd called them, and my mother hadn't said yes until I'd sent a picture of myself to her cell phone to prove I was okay. It had, of course, taken her an hour to find the picture and open it. Cell phone technology still eludes my parents. But in the end, they had agreed to let me stay.

"Never doubt me, Reed," Noelle said blithely, lifting her strawberry kiwi smoothie and taking a sip from the straw. She languidly turned a page of *Vogue* and continued to read. Down the beach, I saw

Paige, Poppy, Sienna, and Daniel, walking along, two by two. My heart caught and I instinctively curled my knees toward my chin, holding my breath as they got closer. One of those girls—most likely crazy little Poppy Simon—was trying to kill me. I was sure of it. Yet they were all friends with Noelle, so I was sure they were going to come over to say hi to her, while being fake-nice to me.

As they approached, I glanced at Noelle, whose eyes were trained on her magazine. I waited for her to look up, to see them and greet them, but she just kept reading. And then . . . they were passing us by. I saw Paige and Sienna whisper to each other, and all four of them quickened their steps and kept walking. My heart pounded in my temples. What was that about? Any normal person would have wanted to get the gossip about the girl who had almost died at the Ryans' annual party. But then, they weren't normal. Maybe they didn't want to hear the gossip because they all knew that Poppy had pushed me, so they already knew all the details. But barring all of that, why didn't they at least stop to say hello to Noelle, their lifelong friend? I breathed in and out as they strolled farther down the beach and out of sight.

Weird. That had been totally, completely weird.

I glanced up the beach again, uncurling my legs. A guy in green board shorts and a white T-shirt was walking along the water. For a moment I thought it was Upton. Perhaps sensing that I wasn't quite ready to talk to him about everything just yet, he'd made some lame excuse to go home and promised to meet us for lunch. But one good squint and I realized I was looking at Sawyer, not Upton. I sat up and raised a hand to wave him down.

Noelle followed my gaze, saw Sawyer, then returned to her reading. As Sawyer turned his steps up the beach, I stood and dusted the
sand off the back of my shorts. He was holding a single miniature
conch shell, which he toyed with as he approached.

"Hey, Reed," he said, squinting one eye. "Noelle."

"What're you doing all the way down here?" Noelle asked.

"I just wanted to come over and see how Reed was doing," Sawyer
said, looking at me. "Feeling better?"

"Yeah," I said. "Still a little sore, but better."

His eyes flicked down at my chest. "Hey. You're wearing the necklace," he said brightly.

Noelle glanced up as my fingers flew to the shell around my neck.
"Yeah. I really like it."

"Cool." Sawyer was blushing. I could feel Noelle's gaze burning
into the back of my neck. "So, do you . . . I mean, are you okay to take
a walk?" Sawyer asked as the wind blew his shaggy blond hair over his
eyes.

"Definitely," I said. I grabbed my sunglasses off the beach blanket
and put them on. I didn't want to get too far away from Noelle's house,
which we were currently parked in front of, but a quick walk with
Sawyer wasn't going to kill me. "We'll be right back."

"I'll be right here," Noelle said, refocusing on the magazine.

Sawyer and I walked down to the wet sand, where cool water lapped
at our feet. He fiddled with his shell as we continued on down the
beach.

"Listen, I wanted to thank you again," I said, biting my lip.

He reddened and shook his head. "You don't have to—"

"No. Not just for the dramatic rescue thing," I said with a laugh. "For saying you believe me about being pushed off the boat."

Sawyer's head snapped up. "I wasn't just saying that. I *do* believe you."

"I know. So thanks. I don't think anyone else really does," I told him, curling my toes into the wet, sloppy sand with each step.

"Not even Upton?" he asked, his voice tight.

"He says he does, but . . ." I looked out at the water. "I think he doesn't want to believe that someone he knows could do that."

"That sucks," Sawyer said. He stopped, turned toward the ocean, and pulled his arm back. With a flick of his wrist he sent the shell flying. It made the tiniest splash out on the water. Then he stood there and stared after it for a long moment, his expression brooding. "After everything you've been through the past couple of years . . . it must just suck when people don't have your back."

My skin prickled and I looked down at my bare toes. I hadn't told Sawyer anything about my . . . history. "I guess people are talking about me, huh?"

Sawyer sighed. "You've been a major topic the last couple of days." He glanced at me quickly as he stooped for another shell to throw. "Sorry."

"No. It's okay," I said, even as my heart squeezed. I hooked my thumbs into the back pockets of my shorts and drew a wide arc in the sand with my toe. It instantly disappeared, sucked away by the salty water. "Bad things just kind of . . . happen to me," I said. "Sometimes

I think there's this big gray cloud following me around. I want it to go away already."

Sawyer nodded. He threw the shell, then drew a long line with his own toe. It disappeared, too. "I feel like that sometimes." He looked up, across the water at the horizon, and tucked his hands under his arms. "I guess you've heard that my sister died a few months ago."

"I did. I'm so sorry," I said, my heart going out to him. Noelle had told me about the Hathaways' loss earlier in the week. "What happened?" As soon as the words were out of my mouth, I heard the presumptuousness of them and wanted to take them back. "I mean, unless you don't want to talk about it. I completely understand if—"

"No. It's fine. I brought it up," Sawyer said flatly. "She killed herself, actually."

My hand covered my heart as I gasped. "What? Why?"

Sawyer looked at me for the first time. "That's the thing. I have no idea," he said, adjusting his arms over his chest, gripping himself even tighter. "She didn't even leave a note."

My hand was over my mouth now. "Omigod, Sawyer. I'm so sorry. That's gotta be so . . ."

"Yeah. It is," he said, nodding again and looking at the ground. "It's the worst part . . . the not knowing."

"God, I know how that feels," I breathed.

Sawyer looked at me. I could feel him wanting to ask what I meant, but unlike me, he knew how to hold his tongue.

"My boyfriend Thomas . . . I'm sure you heard . . . He was killed last year," I said.

"Ariana," Sawyer said.

I froze at the unexpected uttering of her name. For a moment I'd spaced on the fact that she was part of the St. Barths crew. That Sawyer had actually known her.

"Yeah. But before we knew that he was dead, he just went missing. And those few days when I had no idea where he was or why he'd gone or if he was hurt or dead or just avoiding me . . . those were the worst few days ever. Not knowing something that huge is unbearable."

"But you beared it . . . bore it . . . whatever," Sawyer said with a quick laugh.

There was a pang of sorrow in my chest. I had never thought about it that way before. At the time I'd thought there was no way I would ever get through those days. But I had. And I had come out the other side.

"Yeah. I guess I did," I replied with a slight smile.

"My dad always says, 'What doesn't kill you, makes you stronger,'" Sawyer said confidently. Suddenly his whole demeanor changed. He rolled his shoulders back and his chest lifted, as if just saying those words pumped him up from the inside.

"I like that," I said. "If it's true, I should be about as strong as the Hulk by now."

Sawyer laughed and I grinned. I had made the brooding boy laugh. Go me.

"Listen, there's something I want to tell you. Graham said not to, but I think you should know," Sawyer said.

My heart skipped a foreboding beat. "What is it?"

"That night on the boat, Kiran and Taylor realized you and Upton were gone and they started joking around about it. You know, stupid immature crap about where you were . . . what you were doing . . . ," he said, avoiding eye contact.

I blushed and looked away.

"But then all of a sudden, Paige grabbed Daniel and pulled him off the craps table and they were all whispering and stuff and then they just disappeared," Sawyer continued, his words tumbling over one another. "They didn't come back until right before Upton and Poppy did."

I swallowed a huge lump in my throat. So Upton *had* been with Poppy while I was getting almost-killed. What the hell was it with those two?

Focus, Reed. So not the point here.

"So you think . . . I mean, do you think that Paige or Daniel could've been the one who pushed me?" I asked, my voice quavering.

"I don't know," Sawyer replied firmly. "That's all I saw. And five minutes later Upton realized you hadn't come back to the party and we all started searching the boat. Including Paige and Daniel."

I nodded, my heart slamming against my rib cage. I'd never liked the Ryan twins. Never trusted them. Now it seemed like I had a good reason.

"Should I not have told you?" Sawyer asked, his eyes full of worry.

"No. I mean, yes. It's fine," I said. "It's good to know."

For a long moment, I just let this information sink in. I stared out at the water and felt a wall of fear rising up inside my chest. A couple of nights ago I had been out there somewhere, alone and scared and freezing. I had almost died in that ocean. I had always suspected that Poppy might be behind the horse-riding incident and the Jet Ski thing. She was irate that Upton had dumped her and seemed a bit off in general—she'd even disappeared for a couple days without telling anyone. But perhaps I was wrong about her. Was it possible the Ryans were to blame?

"You wanna head back?" Sawyer asked.

I looked up the beach at Noelle. She was watching us from behind her big black sunglasses, keeping an eye on me as promised. I wanted to run over there and tell her what Sawyer had just told me, but I hesitated. What if she said I was crazy? What if she took Paige's side? I so didn't want to deal with being talked down to again.

Part of me wanted to stick close to her, simply because I always felt safe when Noelle was around, but I felt safe here, too. If anything, I felt more comfortable with Sawyer than I did with pretty much anyone else on the island. Not only did he believe my story, but he was actually trying to help me. Going against this stupid "since zygotes" St. Barths cult and telling me the truth.

Besides, not everyone had been through the sorts of losses we had been through. Not Upton, certainly. He thought he was so worldly, but nothing bad had ever happened to the guy. If I was living under a dark cloud, he was basking in the sun. It made him lucky, yes, but when it came down to it, it also made him kind of naive.

What I really needed right then was to be around someone who understood.

"Let's walk a little farther," I said.

"You sure?" Sawyer asked, concerned. "You must be tired."

"I think exercise is probably good for me," I told him, turning my back on Noelle and starting down the beach again. "But let's talk about something else."

"Something nontragic?" Sawyer said with a smirk.

"Nontragic would be perfect," I replied.

SAFE

"Nothing's going to happen to you in a crowded restaurant," Noelle said as we got out of her BMW, which she'd just parked in front of Shutters, the St. Barths crew's favorite hangout. She handed her keys to the valet and walked around the front of the car. Waiting for us under the colorful awning was a whole host of familiar faces. Dash McCafferty, Noelle's maybe-on-again boyfriend, all polo-shirt preppy and blond, stood between Kiran Hayes and Taylor Bell, all of them watching me with a mixture of encouragement and pity. Kiran was wearing a red sundress, her long dark hair tied back in a loose French braid, while Taylor wore a cute madras dress, her blond curls still wet from the shower or the ocean. Upton was talking to Tiffany Goulbourne, gesturing hugely as he told some story that had her laughing. Sawyer, meanwhile, was standing next to Amberly Carmichael, watching me as she chatted his ear off.

"We're all going to get a big table in the middle of the patio," Noelle said, hooking her arm through mine. "You know you can trust *these* guys at least, right?"

I cast a suspicious look at Amberly. She blushed as she noticed her bra strap showing under the boat neck of her light blue dress and she quickly tucked it away.

"Yeah. I guess." I said. But I'd be keeping my eye on the freshman, just in case. If there was one thing I'd learned over the past year, it was that sometimes the most innocent-looking people, the people you never considered, were the most evil people you'd ever encounter. And I already knew Amberly wasn't as sweet as she appeared on the outside. But Noelle was family friends with her, and she was officially in Billings, the dorm I'd be moving back into when we got home, so it appeared I was stuck with her.

"Hi, Reed! How are you feeling!?" Amberly gushed as we approached. She didn't care about me. She just wanted to feel like she was part of the drama.

"Fine," I said, striding right past her.

I might be stuck with her, but that didn't mean I had to be nice.

Taylor, Kiran, and Tiffany rushed over to greet me with hugs and cheek kisses and questions and concerns. Everyone was talking at once, and suddenly I felt completely overwhelmed.

"Come on, people. This isn't a press conference," Noelle said, tugging on my arm. "I'm sure they have our table waiting."

Everyone immediately backed off. Noelle was, as always, in charge. I shot her a grateful look as we walked through the interior lounge area of the restaurant. We were about to hit the outside patio and seating area when Upton fell into step with me.

"You look lovely," he said, planting a kiss on my cheek. "Relaxed."

"Thanks," I replied.

He slipped his hand into mine and entwined our fingers together. Part of me wanted to resist, but his expression was so hopeful, I let him hold on to me. We could talk about our issues later. For now, it felt nice to have his warm fingers clutching mine. Noelle let Upton and me walk ahead while she fell back to walk with Dash. I glanced over my shoulder at them and saw him brush her fingers with his. Noelle pulled her hand away but blushed as she suddenly became very interested in Kiran's new shoes.

Things were finally getting back to normal.

We walked through the open double doors and out onto the patio en masse. The maître d' grabbed a stack of menus and started toward a large round table right at the center of the patio. The slatted roof overhead allowed the sun to pour in over the white linen tablecloth, and all the silverware and glassware gleamed. The scents of Caribbean barbecue filled my senses, and my stomach growled audibly. Once again, I had to concede: Noelle had had a good idea.

Maybe I should just let her run my life from now on.

Upton pulled out a chair for me and I was about to sit when I heard a familiar, cloying laugh. Poppy's laugh. I stood up straight and whirled around. Poppy, Paige, and Sienna were all seated at a small table near the corner, framed by gorgeous tropical flowers bursting from the planters all along the edge of the patio. Sitting there in their designer sundresses, their tan skin gleaming, their heads thrown back in laughter, they would have appeared to any normal person the perfect picture of privileged youth. All I saw was an evil triad of death.

As soon as they saw me, they started to whisper to one another behind their hands. What were they doing? Plotting their next attack?

I shoved the chair aside, stepped around a stunned Upton, and walked over to their table. Their laughing mouths snapped shut as I approached. Paige Ryan looked at me as if I was some kind of straggly half-drowned cat that had just washed up on the beach. She tossed her wavy auburn hair back from her face as she reached for her water goblet.

"Oh. It's you," she said, taking a sip as she looked away.

"Which one of you did it?" I spat, hovering over them. "Which one of you shoved me off that boat?"

The diners at the nearby tables fell silent. Someone's fork clattered to the wooden floor. Sienna's jaw dropped and all three of them exchanged an appalled look.

"Excuse me?" Sienna said in her thick Spanish accent.

"You could have *killed* me!" I shouted, gripping the back of the one empty chair at the table. Piled on it were their colorful Tod's beach bags. I felt Upton walk up behind me, but I didn't turn. I was too focused. "Do you think you're so untouchable? Do you think you can try to murder someone and there won't be any consequences? Which one of you did it? At least have the guts to look me in the eye and tell me!"

Sienna simply stared at me as if she was concerned for my mental well-being. Poppy scoffed and looked away. Paige raised her eyebrows, tilted her head, and took another sip of water. The entire patio was so quiet I could practically hear the ice melting in the glasses at the next table. All of my friends were still standing around our table, staring, clearly unsure of what to do.

"Wow, Upton. You definitely have interesting taste in girls," Paige said, earning a laugh from the other two.

"You know what I think?" Poppy said in her crisp British accent, leaning forward with her elbows on the table. "I don't think you were pushed. I believe you jumped. I believe this whole thing is just a cry for attention. So perhaps you should stop accusing people of something that didn't even happen."

The fingers on my right hand curled into a tight fist. I was so angry my vision actually went hazy. She was going to accuse *me* of making a play for attention? The girl who had disappeared off the island for days, neglected to return hundreds of phone calls from her friends and family, and let everyone think she was dead?

Upton's hand fell on my shoulder. "Reed, perhaps we should just—"

"No!" I blurted, shrugging him off me. "I can't believe you're saying I made this up," I said to Poppy. "Who the hell do you think you are?"

She rolled her eyes and took a bite of her salad.

"Reed," Upton said.

"No! I just want to know. I just want to know who tried to kill me."

"I believe I have the answer to that question," a booming voice announced.

Upton and I turned around to find Mr. and Mrs. Ryan, as well as their son Daniel, striding through the restaurant. Everyone started whispering again as dozens of pairs of wide eyes followed the family's progress across the patio. Mrs. Ryan stood behind her daughter, placing her hands on Paige's shoulders, as Mr. Ryan stepped up next to Upton. Daniel hovered near the corner, as close to Poppy as he could get without falling off the edge of the deck. I was starting to understand the massive crush he had on her. Took a nutter to attract a nutter, apparently.

"What do you mean?" Upton asked.

"Reed, I'm so sorry about this," Mr. Ryan began, turning a piece of paper around in his hands. "As it turns out, the person who attacked you was under our employ."

"What?" Paige blurted.

"You mean she actually *was* pushed?" Poppy asked, her eyes wide.

If Upton hadn't touched my wrist right then, there's a very good chance I would have given her a black eye.

"It was Marquis," Mr. Ryan said.

I blinked, taken aback. Marquis was a nice man who worked as a maître d' at Shutters and occasionally waitered at parties for the Ryans. The members of the St. Barths crew were friendly with him and he'd always seemed perfectly normal. I couldn't believe the man with the welcoming smile and easy laugh had tried to kill me.

"No," Upton said. "We've known him for years. Why would he—"

"It seems his family has fallen on hard times," Mr. Ryan explained. "He was after the necklace. The police found it in his house. We are all so sorry, Reed. As Upton mentioned, we've known the man for years. I never would have thought him capable of something like this."

My mind whirled with the news. If this was true, then no one was trying to kill me. I had just been collateral damage. The runaway horse and the faulty Jet Ski were just accidents, like Upton had said. No one wanted me dead. I was safe. Perfectly safe. Right?

"This is unbelievable," Upton said.

"But it's good news, right?" Noelle said, walking over to us. It seemed everyone in the small restaurant had heard Mr. Ryan's announcement. "I mean, I liked Marquis too, but this means Reed can stay. It means you're safe," she told me. She even spoke slowly, like she was addressing someone who had just learned the language.

"Right," I said. "I guess so."

"Miss Brennan, my husband and I feel responsible. If there's anything we can do to make this up to you, please just ask," Mrs. Ryan said in a formal tone.

I glanced up at her and her beady eyes bored into mine. Suddenly I couldn't help recalling in full detail the last time I had seen her. When she'd caught Upton and me half naked in her stateroom. My face colored and I looked around at the table. Paige, Poppy, and Sienna were all glaring at me. Of course they were. I had just accused them of attempted murder. And as it turned out, I was wrong.

I cleared my throat and wiped my palms on my shorts. "Um . . . I'm sorry about the . . . about what I just said. I guess you guys had nothing to do with it."

So why did I still feel so very uncertain? Sawyer's words niggled at the back of my mind. If Paige and Daniel were innocent, then where had they gone off to that night? Why had they disappeared? But if Marquis had done it, I guess it didn't matter where they'd gone. They must have been off doing something else. It was all just a coincidence.

"Gee, you think?" Paige blurted. "I can't believe you think you can just come over here and—"

"*Paige*," Mr. Ryan said vehemently. In two seconds he'd gone from white with sorrow to red with rage. Paige sank in on herself slightly as she looked up at her father. She cleared her throat and took another sip of water before looking at me again.

"Apology accepted," she said in a clipped tone. "Right, girls?"

Sienna snorted and Poppy's eyes clouded with ire. "Yeah," she said tersely. "Absolutely."

"Thanks," I replied, playing my part in the little charade.

"Come on," Upton said. He took my hand and held it between both of his. "Let's go order."

I nodded mutely and let him and Noelle lead me back to the table. Relief flooded my body with each step, and I felt light as air. It was over. Really and truly over. I could stay on St. Barths after all. I could work things out with Upton and enjoy the rest of break. Finally, *finally* everything was going to be okay.

SO JUVENILE

"We need to talk."

I dropped down on the colorful, striped beach blanket next to Upton's. He laid aside his iPhone and gave me a killer smile. "Well. That sounds ominous," he said.

All around us, our friends were going about usual beach business, chatting, dozing, or racing along the water's edge. After lunch, we had all adjourned to the beach in front of the Simon Hotel, Poppy's parents' establishment. Even the evil triad, as I was now calling them in my mind—although they had apparently *not* tried to kill me—was in attendance. Though they, along with Daniel and Weston Bright, had set up camp a few conspicuous yards up the beach away from the rest of us. I glanced back at them and caught the triad watching me as they whispered to one another, their heads close together. My heart skipped a nervous beat. I knew they were seriously pissed off that I had publicly accused them of attempted murder, and I wondered what they were talking about now—or planning. I hoped that I would not be spending another afternoon locked up in a shower stall . . . or something much worse.

"Everything okay?" Upton asked.

I took a deep breath and turned to face him. I had to try to focus on the task at hand. "Not really."

There was a tiny stick between us in the sand. I picked it up and used it to doodle my name in the soft powder. I knew that if I was going to be staying on in St. Barths, I had to deal with what had happened on the Ryans' boat. So why was there a ball of dread sitting in the center of my stomach?

"It's about casino night," I said, watching the stick as I started a series of curlicues. "You know when Poppy and Mrs. Ryan found us . . ."

"Ah." Upton crossed his legs in front of him. "Let's have it, then."

Did he really not know what he'd done? The thought was so frustrating it immediately crowded out my trepidation.

"You went after Poppy," I said under my breath, glancing back at her to make sure she wasn't in hearing range. Girl was still conspiring with the rest of the evil triad. "Do you have any idea how that felt? I was mortified and you left me there alone and went after your ex."

Upton looked legitimately confused. His brow furrowed and he, too, looked back at Poppy and the others. "You mean after she and Mrs. Ryan came—" Suddenly his face filled with realization and he laughed. "Oh, Reed, I didn't go after Poppy. I went after Paige's mum."

I blinked. "*What?*"

"It's all a proper misunderstanding," he said, lifting my hand and holding it with both of his. "Listen, Mrs. Ryan is good friends with my mum and dad and I just wanted to make sure she wasn't going to go tattling on me. My parents, they're . . . they can be quite old-fashioned sometimes, so if they were to find out what we were doing . . ."

"You were worried about getting in trouble with your parents?" I asked, flabbergasted.

"When you put it that way, it sounds silly, but it was more about you," he said, reaching over to tuck a stray hair behind my ear. "I didn't want them thinking you were, you know, that kind of girl."

He pressed his teeth together in a sort of grimace and I laughed even as I blushed. I didn't exactly care what Upton's parents thought of me, but maybe it was good that Mrs. Ryan and Poppy had stopped us. It gave me more time to consider how far, exactly, I wanted to take this thing with Upton. To figure out if I was really *that kind of girl*.

"So you didn't go off to comfort Poppy. Because Sawyer said that when you came back to the party, you were with her," I told him.

Upton's expression clouded and he hesitated for a second. "Oh. Maybe for a minute, but just for a quick chat. Then I didn't see Poppy again until we boarded a search boat to go out looking for you."

I glanced past Upton's shoulder at Sawyer, who sat on a towel closer to the water, hunched over a tattered novel. He had seemed to think it was more than a quick chat. Was it possible that he had simply inferred something that wasn't actually there? Or was Upton downplaying it on purpose?

"So, are we friends again?" Upton asked, looping one strong arm around my shoulders and pulling me into him. I sighed, happy to be so close to him again.

"I guess I can take you back," I joked.

"I appreciate your benevolence," Upton smirked.

"Gage! Quit it!" Kiran squealed, running up the beach from the water, her long dark hair soaking wet and her tan body beaded with water. Gage Coolidge chased after her with a huge dead crab, its limp legs flapping around as he taunted her with it. Classic immature Gage. Sometimes I wondered why they ever let the guy graduate kindergarten.

"What? The international supermodel is afraid of a little crustacean?" Gage said, holding it out as he lunged for her.

Kiran squealed and whirled away. "Hello? Aren't any of you guys going to save me?"

"I'm on it!" Graham volunteered, tossing the volleyball to Dash. He raced down the beach and charged Gage, tackling him to the sand. The crab went flying and dropped to the ground right at Amberly's feet. She screamed and scampered away on her hands and knees, kicking sand all over Noelle's back as she lay on her towel.

"Amberly! What the hell?" Noelle spat.

"Sorry! He threw a dead thing at me!" Amberly whined.

Noelle rolled her eyes and turned her head away from Amberly. Graham and Gage, meanwhile, laughed, grunted, and trash-talked as they wrestled each other in the sand. Kiran, looking decidedly untraumatized, walked over, grabbed her towel, and dropped down at my other side.

"You know what we need?" she said as Graham shoved Gage's face into the sand with the heel of his hand. She blithely rubbed her hair with the towel. "A party."

"There's a shock," Noelle muttered.

Dash trotted over to join us now that the volleyball teams were uneven, trailing Tiffany and Taylor, who had been playing with the guys. They all stood around in a semicircle, watching as Gage flipped Graham over and pinned him to the ground.

"Nice move, dude!" Dash yelled as he sat.

"No, I'm serious!" Kiran said. She flicked a speck of sand off her flat stomach and leaned back on her elbows, stretching out her perfect bikini body for all to see. "I think we need a New Year's Eve—slash—Thank You, Sawyer, for Saving Reed's Life party."

"You hear that, Sawyer?" Graham shouted to his brother as he pushed Gage off himself and stood. He walked over to Sawyer and dragged him up off his blanket. "Kiran wants to throw you a party!"

Upton picked up the stick I'd been playing with earlier and jabbed it at the sand.

Graham got Sawyer in a headlock and bullied him over to our group. By the time they got there, Sawyer's face was bright red—either from exertion or embarrassment or both.

"You really don't have to do that," Sawyer replied, shoving Graham off him.

Upton tossed the stick at the ground, where it happened to land near Sawyer's feet. I felt a sizzle of tension pass between the two guys.

Was Upton angry that he hadn't gotten to play the hero that night? I nudged him with my shoulder.

"Kiran's right," Upton said quickly, clearing his throat. "A party is definitely in order."

"Woo hoo!" Kiran cheered.

"But New Year's Eve is three days away. Can you really plan a proper party in that time?" Upton asked.

"You *so* underestimate me, Mr. Giles," Kiran joked. She whipped her BlackBerry out of her canvas tote and started dialing. "I'm going to start making arrangements right now."

As Kiran did her party-planning thing, Graham started up with Sawyer and soon a new wrestling match ignited. Gage and Dash both joined in, and before I knew it Upton was on his feet and rushing into the scrum. Even West and Daniel got involved.

"Boys," Noelle said, rolling her eyes as she sat up to watch. "So juvenile."

But of course we all couldn't help watching and laughing as they tossed each other around in the sand. For the first time in days I felt completely happy, completely at ease. I felt like my vacation was just about to start.

AN OFFER

"Aren't you glad you stayed?" Taylor said as we stepped through the automatic sliding doors to the Simon Hotel's gilded lobby the following night for dinner. The marble-tiled floor shone beneath our Jimmy Choos, and almost every surface was bursting with pink and purple blooms. A three-piece band played Caribbean music softly in the corner, the steel drum gonging a happy tune. I took a deep breath of the salt air and smiled. We were there to meet up with the rest of the crew and have dinner at the Simon's most exclusive restaurant. Everyone had dressed up for the occasion. I saw a few heads turn as Taylor and I paused to wait for Kiran and Noelle.

"Yeah. I kind of am," I replied giddily.

"That dress is killer, Reed," Kiran said, stepping up behind me with Noelle. I was wearing a black dress with a halter neck and a slim skirt—a dress Kiran had bought for me our first day on the island—and I did feel rather killer. "Upton's going to have a stroke when he sees you."

"Let's hope not," I replied. "I don't think I can handle a sudden death."

"What do you say we make a pact never to utter the word *death* again," Noelle suggested, lifting her thick brown hair over her shoulder. She was wearing a black strapless dress that made mine look like a muumuu. "At least until we get back to Easton."

"Deal," I replied with a laugh.

"There they are," Taylor said, lifting her chin. The rest of our group was gathered around the lobby bar, their voices gradually growing louder and more jovial, filling the high-ceilinged room. The cool air chilled the bare skin of my arms as I crossed the room, concentrating on not teetering in the four-inch heels Kiran had lent me. The last thing I wanted was for Upton to see me fall flat on my face. But as I stepped up next to Tiffany and Amberly, I realized Upton was nowhere to be found.

"Hey, girls," Tiffany said, lifting a champagne flute. "Grab a glass at the bar."

The three of them obliged while I held back.

"Hey, Tiff, where's Upton?" I asked.

"Lounge," Tiffany said, nodding to a wide doorway across the way. "But I don't know if you want to go in there."

"Why not?" I asked, my heart thumping extra hard.

"He's with Poppy," she replied, lowering her voice.

A slick of dread washed down my spine, but I shoved it aside. Somehow Poppy always seemed to manage to corner Upton. But I wasn't just going to stand there and wait for them to come back.

I was going to go get my man. Show her I was not about to be intimidated.

"Thanks." I tucked my black clutch under my arm, strode purposefully across the lobby. Suddenly four-inch heels were not an issue. Adrenaline can be such a fabulous thing.

Leather chairs dotted the lounge and several older men smoked cigars near yet another bar. The lighting was darker in here and it took a moment for my eyes to adjust, but when they did I saw Upton and Poppy standing in the corner near a grand piano, arguing.

"If you think I'm just going to take this you are absolutely mad," Poppy said, her expression incredulous.

"Then I suppose I'm mad," Upton replied, resting his hand on the piano.

"Everything okay?" I asked loudly, walking over to them.

Poppy whirled around at the sound of my voice. Her one-shouldered dress was covered with colorful swirling stripes. I suppose it was made by some famous designer, but it looked like something I could get at Target for $14.99.

"I wish I had never laid eyes on you," she snapped at me, striding past. Then she paused and turned around to face me. "Just so we're clear, that wasn't a death threat, Miss Paranoia. I don't want the coppers to come banging down my door."

Then she laughed and walked away. Through the open door, I saw Daniel make a beeline for her. He reached for her in a solicitous way, but she raised her hand and kept walking, completely blowing him off. Daniel's jaw clenched. Then he turned around and drove his fist into one of the columns near the wall. I flinched as a few people nearby yelped in surprise. Then Daniel took off out the back door of the hotel, his hand tucked under his arm.

"What was that all about?" I asked.

"That was Daniel not controlling his infamous temper," Upton replied, placing his hands on my shoulders from behind. "You look gorgeous, by the way," he said in my ear, sending a thrill down my side. He kissed my shoulder and nuzzled my neck. Suddenly, all I could think about was getting him alone. This guy had a major effect on my insides.

But I couldn't let myself get distracted.

"Thanks," I replied, turning around. "But I wasn't talking about Daniel. What were you and Poppy arguing about?"

Upton put his arms around my waist and pulled me closer. "She's just cross because I backed out of a fund-raiser. It's this thing in London her parents throw every spring, and I'd said I'd take her, but I can't."

"Why not?" I asked.

Upton raised his eyebrows in surprise. "Do you really have to ask?"

I blushed. "Answer please," I joked.

"Well, if you must know, I have a feeling I'm not going to be going out on many dates with other girls from now on," he said, running his fingertip down my cheek. "After you, everyone else would be sodding boring. I couldn't bear it."

I grinned uncontrollably. "Really?"

"Really," he replied.

I couldn't believe it. Upton the ultimate player was actually going to stop playing . . . because of *me*. My heart fluttered in my chest like a hyper butterfly.

Upton leaned down and touched his lips to mine. It was a deep kiss. Full of meaning and intent and mushy emotions I would normally get lost in. But this time, I couldn't stop . . . *thinking*. Did canceling a date three months from now mean that he wanted to stay together? That he wanted to do a long-distance thing? Could a lifelong player like himself really go from sixty to zero that quickly? Before long I found myself pulling away from him.

"That's really sweet, Upton, but . . ."

"But what?" he asked.

"You're going to be in England and I'll be in Connecticut," I said, lifting a shoulder. "I don't expect you to be my long-distance boy-friend."

"What if I want to be?" Upton asked without hesitation, pushing his hands into his pockets.

Yes. Yes, yes, yes. That was all I wanted to say in that moment. Upton was so much more mature than the guys I was used to. So easygoing and drama free (if you didn't count his crazy exes). I would have loved to have had a long-term boyfriend like him. He made me feel safe and loved and most of all . . . carefree. He saw the world as full of possibility, and he made me see it that way too.

But then my rational side kicked in. Maybe Upton had told me he was falling in love with me, but I didn't exactly expect that to translate into a future for us. It was great that he was offering to be my one and only, but what if he went back to England and realized he couldn't do it? Even if he didn't, I knew I'd always be suspicious. Did I really want to be hanging out at Easton, all celibate and alone, wondering where he was at every moment . . . and with whom?

"Can I think about this?" I asked. "It's kind of a new concept for me."

"Take all the time you need," Upton said, reaching for my hand with a smile. He seemed pretty confident that I'd eventually agree. "In the meantime, I was thinking we should do something fun together tomorrow. Something that will get our minds off everything that's happened in the last few days."

"I don't know. Every time we do something fun I almost end up dead," I said, only half joking.

Upton laughed as we walked back into the lobby together. "Are you turning me down?"

"Not exactly," I said, swinging our hands between us. "What if we just do something chill? Lay low for a day."

Upton paused and looked at me in a suggestive way. "*Lay* low? I like the sound of that."

"Ha-ha," I said flatly. "You're hilarious."

He pulled me to him and gave me another quick, firm kiss. "Whatever you want," he said, looking me in the eye. "I'm there. The next few days . . . they're all about you."

BREAKFAST DATE

I didn't sleep all night. All I could think about were Upton and his proposal. This thing with him was supposed to be just a vacation fling. Nothing more. Something fun to pass the time. Yes, I had developed feelings for him over the past week. Serious feelings. But were they the kind of feelings that could sustain a long-distance relationship? A relationship that would span a whole ocean? Separate continents? Different time zones?

And what about Josh? Yes, I knew he was with Ivy, but the last time I'd seen him he'd implied—practically stated—that he still loved me. If there was a chance that he and I could be together, did I really want to risk that?

Wait. No. I wasn't just going to sit around like a loser and wait for Josh to wake up and smell the true love. He hadn't even called me or texted me once since I'd been here. Not even on Christmas Day.

But if I stayed with Upton, when would I ever see him? Holidays? Long weekends? I knew what my friends would say. I was only sixteen. Now was not the time to become a nun.

When my phone beeped at 6 a.m., I was so excited for a distraction I fell out of my bed reaching for it.

The text was from Sawyer, the message simple:

Shutters for bfast? 7?

Oh, I was so in. If I didn't get out of this room soon, I was going to start clawing the stucco walls, which would seriously screw up the French manicure Taylor had given me after I'd gotten out of the hospital. Maybe Sawyer would even have some advice for me. He knew Upton, and he seemed like a levelheaded guy. This could be exactly what I needed. I texted back.

Im there!

I showered quickly and dressed in a simple blue skirt and white T-shirt, bringing along my hoodie just in case. My hair was still slightly damp when I padded through the door of Shutters an hour later in my flip-flops, having borrowed one of the Langes' mopeds to get myself there. (Waking up Noelle for her car keys was not an option. Unless I wanted to lose a limb.)

The restaurant was dotted with diners, mostly couples, but not nearly as crowded as it would be in a couple of hours when the regulars would roll in for their breakfast. Sawyer was sitting at the corner table that Poppy, Paige, and Sienna seemed to prefer, and for once, his face wasn't bent toward a book. He was watching the door intently and stood up when I arrived. His black T-shirt was as wrinkled as if he'd slept in it, and his cargo shorts hung loosely on his thin frame. As always, his blond hair was brushed forward toward his face.

"Can I help you?" the maître d' asked.

"Just meeting a friend," I said, gesturing in Sawyer's direction.

The man smiled and I wove my way around the tables to join Sawyer. The morning breeze was oddly cool and almost crisp. I untied my sweatshirt from around my waist and pulled it on.

"Hey, Reed. Thanks for coming," Sawyer said, sitting only after I had seated myself.

"No problem. Is everything okay?" I asked.

"Yeah, fine," Sawyer said. He stuffed his hands under his arms and hunkered down in his chair, trying to escape the wind. "I just couldn't sleep."

"Me neither!" I replied, perhaps a bit too manically. For some reason, when I don't sleep, I seem to have a ton of energy. At least first thing in the morning.

"Really?" Sawyer's face lit up. Misery loves company. "Does that happen to you a lot?"

"Not a lot," I replied.

Only when people are missing, or someone's stalking me, or all my friends stop talking to me, or a sexy video of me gets sent out to my entire school, or some guy I like asks me to be his long-distance girlfriend. So yeah. Hardly ever.

"Oh." He seemed disappointed. "It happens to me all the time."

The waiter delivered our menus and I set mine aside. After eat-

ing here practically every morning of the trip, I had the thing memorized.

"I was having deep thoughts," I confessed, crossing my arms on
the tabletop.

Sawyer raised his eyebrows as he looked up from his menu. "About
what?"

"Upton," I replied.

"Oh." He looked down again and set the menu aside. When his
eyes met mine, there was something guarded in them, even as he
attempted to smile. "What about him?"

"He wants me to be his long-distance girlfriend," I told him. "He
wants me to . . . commit."

"You don't want to do that," Sawyer said firmly. He didn't even
hesitate. It was as if the words had been on the tip of his tongue for
days, just waiting to vault out.

"I don't?" I asked.

"It's crap. Upton doesn't commit. It's not in his DNA," Sawyer
replied.

"But he—"

"Trust me," Sawyer said in a no-nonsense tone. "Sure, he cares
about you now. In the moment he's all about whoever he's with. But a
girl like you . . . you're too good for him. You don't want to get in any
deeper with Upton Giles. You're just going to end up hurt."

The way he said Upton's name made it sound like an insult. Like
he was talking about some gross venereal disease. My face started to
burn. I might have been uncertain about committing to a transatlantic

relationship, but that didn't mean I didn't care about Upton. That I didn't think he was a good person. Yet here Sawyer was, insulting the guy to my face. Judging both of us, really.

The waiter came and took our orders. My hand trembled as I handed the menu back to him. There was a hot, frustrated anger bubbling under the surface of my skin, but Sawyer seemed oblivious. He took a sip of his water and crunched on an ice cube, leaning back in his chair.

"How do you know what kind of girl I am?" I asked.

Sawyer blinked. "What?"

"You barely know me," I said, trying to keep my voice steady. "How do you know what kind of girl I am? Maybe I *am* the kind of girl who wants to get in deeper with a guy like Upton. Who, by the way, has been nothing but sweet to me since I got here."

My words hung in the air between us. Sawyer just sat there, staring at me. He didn't blush or stammer or squirm. He didn't move a muscle.

"Sorry," he said finally. "You're right. I don't know you."

I had no idea what to say next, but suddenly I didn't feel like being there anymore. So much for a chat with Sawyer making me feel better. My foot bounced up and down under the table, expending some of my pent-up energy. I looked away and lifted my glass, preoccupying myself with a long sip.

"Are you mad?" he asked.

"No," I replied. A knee-jerk no.

"You're mad." He let out a sigh. I had yet to look at him again, but I heard him scoot his chair forward and, from the corner of my eye, saw him lean his torso into the table. "Don't be mad. I'm sorry. It's just . . . you remind me so much of her, I guess I just assumed—"

"Who do I remind you of?" I asked, finally meeting his gray eyes.

Sawyer's face flooded with color. "No one. Forget it."

"No. There's no 'forget it' now," I said. "Who do I remind you of?"

He brought one hand to his forehead, pushing his thick bangs aside. "My sister. You remind me of Jen."

My skin prickled, wondering what that meant, exactly. The waiter delivered our food—a neat stack of fruit-topped pancakes for me, scrambled eggs for Sawyer—but I didn't even look at it. Sawyer held my gaze for a brief moment, but the effort was too much for him. He glanced away.

"It's just really hard, being here without her," Sawyer said, looking out at the ocean. "I didn't want to come, but everyone insisted. And then seeing you . . . and you with him . . ."

My heart contracted. "Was Jen with Upton?"

Sawyer scoffed. His eyes looked glassy. "Everyone has been with Upton at some point."

I knew this. Of course I knew this. It was all I had heard since before I'd met the guy. But my stomach turned nonetheless. Upton had been with Jen Hathaway. Sometime in the recent past, I had to assume, since it still stung Sawyer. A girl Upton had been with was dead. Had committed suicide.

Maybe he knew more about tragedy than I imagined.

"Anyway, I'm sorry," Sawyer said. "I didn't invite you here for this.

I thought . . . I just thought it would be cool to hang out. You know, without everyone else."

I took a deep breath. It was well past time to change the subject. I was grateful for the opening. "You're not big on crowds, huh?"

"Hate them," Sawyer said with a small, but wry, smile. "Especially this one. I've known them since I was a kid, but I've never felt like they wanted me around."

"Hmm . . . I've been getting that too," I said.

"Jen made it easier," Sawyer told me, lifting his knife. He paused. Both of us were moving slowly, as if tentatively testing the waters to make sure we wanted to continue in each other's company. "She always figured out a way to get me involved."

"Siblings can be good like that," I said, thinking of my own brother, Scott, who had always let me hang out with his friends even when he thought I was a raving dork. I wondered how this trip might have been different if Jen were here. Whose side would she have taken? Paige, Poppy, and Sienna hadn't spoken to me once at dinner last night. Hadn't even looked in my direction. I wondered if Jen would have sided with them and given me the cold shoulder, or if she would have been okay with me and Upton.

If Sawyer was right—if Jen and I were anything alike—I liked to think she would have been on my side.

"That's why I was so surprised when Kiran had the idea for this party. I thought she didn't know I existed," Sawyer said as he reached for the butter. "I'm kind of nervous about it, actually."

"Nervous?" I said. "Why?"

"No one's ever thrown a party for me before," he replied, blushing. "And I'm not big on the spotlight."

"Oh. Yeah. I get that." I cut into my pancakes as a stiff breeze caused the tropical flowers to dance in their planters. My shoulders started to relax. For a minute there I'd gotten so embroiled in the drama, I'd forgotten where I was, but now the fresh air rushed over me. Soothed me. "Don't worry. I'll make sure they don't get too crazy."

"Yeah?" Sawyer asked hopefully.

"Yeah," I replied. "I mean, I still think you deserve a party, but it can be more like a soiree and less of a—"

"A brouhaha?" he asked.

"I was thinking hootenanny, but we can go with yours," I joked.

Sawyer laughed and the last of the tension melted away from the table. Obviously he was still dealing with some strong emotions about his sister's death, so I wasn't about to hold a grudge about the things he'd said. I understood how that could happen. I was sure I'd said and done some regrettable things after Thomas had died. There was something reassuring about hanging out with someone who understood the dark side of things. Who wouldn't judge me if ever I suffered from verbal vomit.

I had a feeling that Sawyer and I were going to be really good friends.

STORYTELLING

I gripped the underside of my seat as the sailboat tipped sideways and sea spray showered over me, stinging the bare patches of skin. My heart lurched as we tipped even further and I looked down at my life vest. Was this skimpy little thing really going to keep me afloat when we capsized?

"It's beautiful out here today!" Upton shouted as he raced from one side of the boat to the other, turning this crank and adjusting that rod. He wasn't even wearing a vest. What if he slipped and fell overboard? Then I'd be stranded on this boat all alone with no idea how to turn it around and save him. What the hell was he thinking, bringing me out here? What had I been thinking when I said yes? We should have been spending the day on the beach, where it was nice and dry and solid and safe.

"Having fun yet?" he asked jovially, hanging on to a sail line and swinging back and forth.

I forced myself to look out at the water, trying to see this beauty he was so hopped up about, but all I could see was me. Alone. Floating. Sinking. Almost drowning.

That was it. Forget this 'brave Reed' act. I couldn't take it anymore.

"How much longer are we going to be out here?" I asked.

"What?" Upton replied.

"I don't think I can do this!" I shouted, my knuckles smarting from the force of my grip.

Upton's face paled. He seemed to really *see* me for the first time on our sail. He dropped down onto the gleaming wood deck and teetered his way over to me, hanging on to whatever ropes were in reach.

"Are you all right?" he asked, crouching in front of me.

"If this is your idea of lying low . . ."

Upton covered his eyes with his hand, then slid it down to cover his mouth. He looked stricken. "I'm so sorry," he said. "I should have realized. To me this is relaxing, but obviously to you . . . I'm such an idiot."

I didn't say anything to refute this conclusion.

"I was going to anchor the boat out here for a little while," he said. "But if you want to go back—"

"Anchor?" I said, my voice a squeak. "As in stop moving?"

"That's generally what an anchor does, yeah," he joked.

"I think I could maybe handle that."

"All right, then. We'll try it," he said. "But if you want to go back, just say the word."

"Thanks," I said, already feeling more secure. "I will."

Fifteen minutes later, the boat was at rest. Aside from the gentle lolling as it dipped up and down with the waves, there was no movement. Upton helped me up from my perch at the center of the boat and gripped me tightly as I walked on quaking legs to the stern. The area was lined with benches covered with colorful striped cushions. There was a picnic basket, filled with gourmet breakfast foods no doubt, in the center of the wood-paneled floor. I had yet to tell Upton about my early breakfast with Sawyer, figuring that if Sawyer had such negative feelings about Upton, then Upton might feel the same way about Sawyer.

"Is this okay?" Upton asked as I sank onto the soft bench.

"This'll work," I replied, my voice steady.

Upton sat down next to me and put his arm around my shoulders. I curled against him, my bulky life vest shifting awkwardly toward my opposite shoulder. His chest rose and fell steadily beneath my cheek, and I could just make out the beating of his heart. He ran his fingers back and forth over my upper arm and I sighed.

"Yeah. This will definitely work."

Upton shifted and I tilted my head back so I could see him. He moved his fingers to my face and looked into my eyes intently, like he was trying to make out each and every fleck of color there. I smiled slightly and he leaned in to kiss me. The waves lapped at the underside of the boat. Off in the distance, a motor revved, and seagulls cawed overhead. I was no longer scared. We were alone out here, yes, but it didn't matter. Because Upton was with me.

The kiss grew deeper and I gripped Upton's shirt in my hand, pulling him closer to me. The stupid life vest was like a wall between our chests, and when I felt him fumbling for the buckles, I didn't stop him. Forget safety. All I wanted was to feel Upton's body as close to mine as it could get.

The buckles loosened. I flung one arm out of the vest, then sat up, pushing him back momentarily, to free myself from the other. The second the vest hit the floor, Upton nudged me back onto the cushions. Back, back, back until I was lying flat beneath him. He pulled away from our kiss for a moment to look me in the eye again. Make sure I wasn't ready to stop. I so wasn't. He smiled and kissed me again, resting his full weight over my body.

I wrapped my arms around him, pushed my hand up under the back of his shirt so I could feel his skin, which was insanely warm. Upton trailed kisses across my cheek and down my neck. His lips tickled my skin and I turned my head to the side so he could keep going. He brushed my hair away from my shoulder and traced a little circle on my skin with the tip of his tongue. It sent shivers right through me and I laughed.

Upton lifted his head and looked at me quizzically. "Miss Brennan, this is not a laughing matter," he said with mock seriousness.

"Sorry," I said, sliding away from him and sitting up a bit. I crooked one leg over the side of the bench and bent the other on the cushion. "I'll try to be more discreet."

"Good. Because laughter can really mess with a guy's confidence, you know?" he said, still joking.

He picked up my ankle and rested my leg over his lap. Then he started running his fingertips up and down my shin. I bit my lip.

"No laughing," he admonished.

I pressed my lips together. His fingers moved higher, tickling my knee. This was torture.

"No laughing," he warned again.

He moved his fingers higher, caressing my bare thigh. Every inch of my skin grew hot. He looked at me. I wasn't about to laugh. His fingers climbed higher. And higher. I felt them graze the hem of my shorts, but I didn't take my eyes off his. He shifted his position and slipped his hand under the fabric. Higher. Higher. Laughter was no longer an issue.

I wanted to do this. Wanted to let him touch me. But at the last second, something snapped.

"Upton."

He drew his hand away instantly. "I'm starting to sense a pattern here." He wasn't angry. Just disappointed.

"I'm sorry, I just . . ."

Ever since my conversation with Sawyer that morning, I couldn't stop thinking about Jen Hathaway. When, exactly, had she been with Upton? How did she fit into the ever-expanding tangled mess of his love life? And if I looked like her, if I reminded Sawyer so much of her, did Upton see the resemblance as well?

I didn't really want to ask him any of these things. Wasn't sure if I wanted to know the answers. But they just joined the growing list of unknown facts about Upton's past. His very, very colorful past.

Upton studied my face. I didn't know what to say, so I just looked back at him.

"Can I ask you something?" he said finally.

"Okay."

"Would this be . . . I mean, it's not your . . . Would this be your first time?" he asked.

"No," I told him. My face burned and I looked down at my lap. I tugged down on the hems of my shorts. "But it would be my second."

"Oh." He sat back against the cushions. My leg was still across his lap. I was glad he didn't feel the need to move it.

"And it's not that I don't want to, because I do," I said. "It just feels like a big decision, and there's a lot involved. I mean, you've been with *so* many girls and I—"

"Is that what this is about?" Upton said. "You're still jealous."

"No! Not jealous," I said, sitting forward. "I swear it's not that. I'm just . . . curious. About what you've done. And maybe a little worried. I mean, you have a lot of experience and I have *no* idea what I'm doing."

Upton let out a short laugh. A knowing laugh. "We've all been there."

Not exactly the response I was expecting. Or hoping for. I wanted him to say that it didn't matter. That he knew it would be great with me. That every other girl he'd ever been with actually sucked at it, and he was sure I would be amazing. Is it wrong for a girl to want to hear a little white lie at a moment like this?

"What do you mean?" I asked.

"Let me tell you a little story," Upton said, turning sideways on the bench to better face me. Intrigued, I curled my legs up story style. "About my first time."

Interesting. I wasn't sure if I wanted to hear this. But then, he had offered so little detail of his romantic past, and all I'd done was imply that I wanted to know. If I stopped him, I'd look even more immature and squeamish than I already did. So I bit my tongue and said nothing. Bring on the awkwardness!

"It was with an older woman," he said, an amused smile playing on his lips.

"Older like *older*?" I asked. Already I didn't like this.

"Yeah. As in I was a teenager and she was an adult."

Ew. "Okay."

"Talk about being worried about being good," Upton said, shaking his head. "I was terrified. It took me ages just to get up the guts to come out of the bathroom."

I got a mental image of Upton, scrawny and half naked, cowering in a bathroom somewhere while this voluptuous older woman in red lingerie smoked a cigarette in bed, waiting for him. It all seemed so predatory and weird.

"But I finally did and there she was, totally naked, except for this big necklace made out of these sharp, gold leaves, which, for some reason, she neglected to take off," he said with a laugh. "Now I'm both too scared and too polite to say anything, so I just go with it. And the whole time, I'm trying to concentrate and not do anything stupid and make sure I'm respectful, and the whole time, this sodding heavy necklace keeps whacking me in the face. It was a nightmare."

He was laughing full out now, so I forced myself to smile.

You wanted to know this stuff, Reed. You wanted to know where he's been.

"But of course by the time it was all over I didn't mind it anymore. I thought I was so cool and mature when it was done, you know? I was such a little twit." Upton said, shaking his head. "So I go striding back into the bathroom like I'm some kind of experienced playboy now, and I take one look in the mirror and I have dozens of these tiny little cuts all over my face. I had to tell my parents I was attacked by a cat."

"Did they believe you?" I asked, incredulous.

"Who knows? If they didn't, they never told me." Upton settled back in his seat and rested his arm on the back of the cushions. He tickled my shoulder with his fingertips. "So what about you?"

"Me?" I asked, trying to eradicate all the disturbing visuals from my mind.

"What was your first time like?" he asked.

I thought of Thomas and my heart flipped over and died, just like it did every time I got a vivid picture of his face. Those teasing blue eyes. The tiny scar on his jaw. His private just-for-me smile.

"It was nothing as interesting as the story you just told," I said, looking down at my hands.

"Come on. I told you mine, now you tell me yours," Upton chided.

I took a deep breath. "It was sweet. It was perfect, really." I smiled slightly, remembering how cautious Thomas had been with me. How slow and almost reverent. My heart suddenly ached at the thought of him. "It wasn't something I was expecting to do that night, but for once I let go and just did what I wanted to do in the moment. And then a couple weeks later . . . he died."

Upton's eyes clouded over. "Oh, God, Reed, I'm sorry. I'm such an idiot. I'd forgotten."

He looped his arm around my shoulder and pulled me to him, kissing my forehead. "We don't have to talk about this."

"Okay."

He held me there for a long while. I breathed in and out, in and out, until the images went away. Until the aching subsided. I didn't want to be this person. This dark and gloomy person who ruined a perfectly gorgeous day out on the Caribbean Sea talking about her doomed first love with the guy she was currently dating. I wanted to move on. I wanted to be free of the whole thing already. I just wanted to be able to let myself go with Upton. Be completely and truly with him and no one else. Why couldn't I just do that?

"Forget this crap," Upton said suddenly, leaning back to look into my face. "Who wants to talk about awkward, meaningless, stupid first times? All that really matters is *our* first time. Which, by the way, does not have to happen anytime soon. I'm just letting you know that *that* is the only time I care about."

I laughed at his rambling as a stiff wind blew my hair back from my face. I rested my palm on his chest and toyed with the button near his collar. He was right. The ishy encounter with this older woman . . .

whatever I had with Thomas . . . it didn't matter. Those moments had nothing to do with us. And neither did any of the other girls Upton had been with. They couldn't touch us.

I took a deep breath and decided to live in the moment. To not think about the past. To concentrate on how I felt about Upton *right now*. And how I felt, lying there in his arms, was perfectly happy. I knew that he cared about me. He had done so much for me—telling off Poppy, putting together that insane Christmas gift, spending all this time with me over the last week when he could have been hanging out with his friends, not to mention saving my life that day Misty had been spooked. He wanted to be with me. His actions showed that. And I wanted to be with him. More than anything I just wanted to go on feeling this safe, this loved, this blissful.

I felt words bubble up inside of me. I thought about holding them back. But I was letting go.

"What about tomorrow night?" I asked, my voice thick. I looked up at him and wondered if he could feel my heart pounding through both our shirts.

"Tomorrow night?" He was, unsurprisingly, shocked.

"After Kiran's party," I said, sounding completely certain even to my own doubting ears.

"Are you sure?" he asked.

"I figure if you're going to be my long-distance boyfriend, we should probably seal the deal before we go home," I said faux-casually.

Upton's grin lit his entire face. The entire boat. The entire ocean. "I'm going to be your boyfriend, then?"

"If the offer is still on the table," I replied with a smile.

"Oh, it's still on. It's definitely still on," he said. He leaned in and gave me a brief, joyous kiss. "But if we're going to do this, we're going to do it proper-like."

"What do you mean?" I asked, giggling.

"Don't worry about it. I'll take care of everything," he said, leaning back again.

I cuddled into him, resting my cheek against his chest. He ran his hand over my hair and I sighed, feeling content in my decision. Feeling secure. And more than a little bit excited.

Upton kissed the top of my head and I could hear the smile in his voice as he said, "I'm going to make sure that tomorrow is a night neither one of us ever forgets."

DISINVITATION

"What're you going to wear to the party tomorrow?" Kiran asked, taking a sip of her mango guava smoothie.

The two of us were sitting side by side on the stone patio at the Ryans' palatial estate along with Noelle and Taylor, our legs dangling in the crystal-clear infinity pool. Dash, Gage, Graham, and West were all messing around in the water, splashing us occasionally, while Sawyer sat under a teal umbrella, his nose buried in Jean-Paul Sartre's *No Exit*. Amberly and Tiffany were inside, having gone in search of more drinks a few minutes earlier. Paige, Poppy, and Sienna reposed on lounge chairs behind us, pretending to read magazines, even though I could feel them glaring at me over the tops of the pages. They'd invited us over after Upton and I had gotten back from our boat trip, pretending it was a sort of peace offering. But if they were going to launch some kind of attack, I wished they would just get it over with already. Constantly paranoid was not a state I liked to be in.

"I haven't really thought about it," I lied, lifting a shoulder.

My New Year's Eve wardrobe had been one of the many things I'd been obsessing about ever since I'd decided that I was going to have my first time with Upton. I wanted to look sexy, but not trashy. Sophisticated, but not trying too hard. Part of me wanted to go shopping for something brand-new, but unlike my friends, I was completely broke. I'd probably just fall back on the dress Kiran had bought me that I hadn't worn yet—a red minidress with spaghetti straps and a straight neckline. It seemed like a solid choice.

"Big mistake," Kiran said, lifting a hand near her shoulder. "Don't you know that whatever you're wearing when you ring in the New Year sets the tone for the *entire* year?"

"What is that, some kind of supermodel Zen?" Noelle asked, lifting her thick hair over her shoulder and leaning back on her elbows. She tipped her face toward the sun and let her hair dangle to the ground.

"No! It's a proven fact," Kiran replied, dead serious. "When I was twelve I wore Marchesa on New Year's Eve, and that's the year I signed my first modeling contract. But remember what I was wearing junior year?"

Taylor narrowed her eyes behind her frameless Michael Kors sunglasses. "Wasn't that the year you were in the hospital getting your tonsils out?"

"Yes! Exactly! Poly-blend hospital nightgown and paper slippers. And, as we all know, that year sucked like no year has ever sucked before," Kiran said, taking a long, cheek-hollowing sip from her straw. Then she set her glass down and sat up, her posture model perfect. "Make sure you dress appropriately, Reed. If anyone needs a good year, it's you."

"Thanks," I replied, looking down at my feet as I circled them in the water. "I'll keep that in mind."

"Who had the banana mango?" Amberly asked as she and Tiffany returned from the house.

"That would be me," I said, looking up at them. From the corner of my eye, I saw Poppy and Paige whispering again and my heart dropped like a stone. "You guys . . . can I ask you something? It's about Casino Night."

An uncomfortable silence descended. Guess they thought that was a night I wouldn't want to talk about anytime soon.

"What's up?" Tiffany asked finally, settling in next to Kiran.

"It's just . . . I heard that Paige and Daniel mysteriously disappeared from the casino right around the time I was . . . you know." I paused, letting the wave of dread and fear crash over me and pass. "Do you guys remember that at all?"

"Why? I thought they already arrested Marquis," Amberly said. "I thought he confessed and everything."

"He did," Noelle replied. "You've gotta let this go, Reed."

"I know, I know. It's just, those three have been talking about me behind my back and it's starting to drive me crazy," I said, glancing over my shoulder at the evil triad. They saw me and quickly turned away from each other. "I was just wondering . . ."

"Actually, they did leave," Taylor said, putting her glass down.

"What?" Noelle said.

"They did?" My heart began to race.

"I remember it because Daniel was right in the middle of a winning streak at craps and Paige totally pulled him away. Remember?" Taylor said to Kiran. "You had to finish his roll."

"I remember crapping out," Kiran said bitterly.

"They were gone for a while," Taylor said, looking at the others. "I don't even remember seeing them again until we were all going out to search for Reed."

Once again, my friends fell silent. I felt sick to my stomach and set my untouched smoothie aside. Where had Paige and Daniel gone? Had the police arrested the wrong man? But they *had* found the necklace. Then again, how hard would it have been to plant it there?

Suddenly I heard a shout from inside the house and everyone on the patio except the cavorting boys in the pool turned to look. Someone was yelling. *Two* someones. And I realized with a start that one of them was Upton. I couldn't make out what he was saying, but a sudden crash startled everyone to their feet.

"What the hell?" Paige blurted, jumping up from her chair.

She raced across the patio area to the wall of glass doors that fronted her living room. The rest of us were right on her heels. As we walked inside, the frigid, air-conditioned air hit me like a slap to the face. On the floor was a hammered-metal vase, the big yellow flowers it used to hold strewn in an arcing pattern across the tile. Upton and Daniel were facing off in the middle of the living room, and Daniel was red with rage.

"Just give it to me and I might not kick your ass!" Daniel said, holding out his hand.

"Daniel, calm down," Upton replied calmly but firmly. In his hands was a bottle of wine, clearly the object of their contention.

"You guys, what's going on?" Paige demanded. They completely ignored her.

"Don't tell me to calm down!" I flinched as Daniel kicked the metal vase clear across the room like a soccer ball. "You think you can just walk into someone's house and take whatever you want? You're so fucking entitled?" he shouted, the veins on his neck protruding. "Not everything belongs to you, man!"

Poppy looked around at us with an apologetic, but somehow proud, expression. We all knew that Daniel was talking about her more than the bottle of wine.

"I told you, I didn't take it," Upton replied, holding the bottle out to the side. "Your mother gave it to me."

"Yeah, right," Daniel shot back. "Mother would never part with that vintage. That bottle's worth two thousand dollars."

"What do you want me to tell you, mate?" Upton asked, with a shrug. "Ask her yourself."

Daniel's jaw clenched. "Give me the bottle, Upton."

"No," Upton replied.

"This is the last time I'm going to ask. Give. Me. The bottle," Daniel said, advancing on him.

"What are you going to do? Hit me?" Upton asked.

Daniel pulled his arm back and did just that. The crack of fist against jaw sounded like a baseball bat shattering into pieces off a fastball. An involuntary screech escaped my throat and was echoed by the surprised shrieks of every other girl in the room. Upton wheeled around but didn't fall, and somehow kept hold of the precious wine bottle. He was just straightening up when Mr. and Mrs. Ryan rushed in from the stairs in the center hall.

"What is going on in here?" Mr. Ryan thundered.

Mrs. Ryan stooped to retrieve her battered vase and held it in front of her at waist level with both hands, almost like a shield. She regarded the flowers on the floor with distaste, as if their fate was upsetting her more than the fight her son was having.

"Upton stole a bottle of wine from the cellar," Daniel replied, spittle flying from his mouth and showering the floor. "I'm just trying to get it back."

"Daniel, Upton did no such thing," Mrs. Ryan said calmly, but in a scolding tone. "I gave him that bottle."

"What?" Daniel asked, his eyes going glassy. "No. You couldn't have. . . ."

Mrs. Ryan stepped up next to Upton like a protective mother hen. "He was down in the cellar looking for ideas for a special occasion he's planning, and I told him to take the bottle."

I felt a hot blush climbing up my neck and onto my face as Noelle glanced at me with a question in her eyes. I knew exactly what the special occasion was, and, as always, it seemed Noelle had figured it out too.

"Now, Daniel, apologize to Upton," Mrs. Ryan said.

Daniel turned and looked at Upton, who merely stood there. To his credit, Upton didn't appear triumphant at all. He merely looked like he wanted this whole ordeal to be over already. Daniel, however, was still the color of tomato sauce.

"It'll be a cold day in hell," he spat.

"Daniel!" his father shouted.

For the first time since I'd met him, Daniel ignored his father completely. He took a step toward Upton, his expression full of ire. "The next time I see you, you'd better be prepared."

"Daniel," his mother said with a gasp, "what is the matter with you?"

But Daniel had already turned on his heel and was striding away. He shoved through a door at the far end of the room and disappeared from sight.

"All right! That's it!" Kiran said, breaking the silence. She stepped away from the group and turned to face us. "That guy is *not* coming to my party."

"What?" Paige blurted. "You've got to be kidding me."

"It's just too much drama," Kiran replied, holding up both hands. "I will not ring in the New Year with a fight. Daniel is out."

"I don't believe this. You're disiniviting people now? What is this, seventh grade?" Paige said with a laugh.

"It might as well be," Kiran said.

Paige crossed her arms over her chest. "Fine. If Daniel's not coming, I'm not coming."

"Me as well," Sienna added, lifting her chin haughtily.

"Fine. All of you stay home," Kiran said, waving a hand in Poppy's direction. "I'm sick of you and your negative vibes anyway."

"Us!?" Poppy screeched, bringing a hand to her chest. "If any-one's brought negative energy to this island it's her!" She pointed a finger at me, leaning forward for emphasis.

"We've so heard this riff already, and I am beyond over it. It's Kiran's party, and if she says you're out, you're out," Noelle told them. "And I, for one, say brava on the decision." She turned to Paige and Daniel's parents while looping her arm around my back. "Mr. and Mrs. Ryan, thanks for a lovely afternoon, but I think you'll agree we should be going now."

Mrs. Ryan pursed her lips. Her curly auburn hair trembled ever so slightly. "Yes. I believe that would be best," she said, glancing at Upton and his bottle of wine.

"Happy New Year, ladies," Noelle said over her shoulder. "Maybe your resolutions should be to quit being such whiny bitches."

Then she tugged me toward the center hall, getting us out of there before either of Paige's parents could react to the fact that their daugh-ter had just been insulted right in front of them in their own home. The other girls, as well as Dash, Gage, West, and the Hathaways, trailed behind us. I suppose they figured they'd better take our side if they wanted in on the party. I heard Upton murmur a few words to the Ryans, then he jogged to catch up with us.

"That went well," he said facetiously.

"Whatever. I'm sick of their crap," Noelle replied. "If they're gonna dish it, they better be ready to take it."

Then she shoved open the heavy door and we all stepped out into the sunshine.

KISS BUSINESS

"All right, people! We have business to discuss!"

Kiran and Taylor emerged on the patio outside the great room at Noelle's house, several flutes of champagne in hand. Amberly rushed forward in her slinky pink dress to relieve them of a couple of the glasses and passed one to Tiffany. Kiran handed one to me and left one on a glass-topped side table next to Noelle, who was checking her eyebrows in a compact mirror as the sun set over the ocean.

"Business? I thought this was a pre-party party!" Tiffany replied, taking a swig of her champagne.

"It is. But we need to figure out who will be kissing whom at midnight," Taylor said with a wicked grin. She plucked a caviar-and-toast-point hors d'oeuvre from the silver platter on the table and popped it into her mouth. "You know, just so there's no confusion."

"Well, we all know who Reed will be kissing," Tiffany said, slinging her arm around my neck.

They all made the obligatory smoochy noises until my face was about to sear off my head. I adjusted the thin strap on my red dress and turned to look out at the ocean, waiting for the blush to subside. But now, all I could think about was Upton and how we planned to take it way beyond the kissing-at-midnight stage tonight, and the blush became permanent.

"Well, don't any of you bitches get any ideas about Dash," Noelle said.

"Obviously," Kiran said, rolling her eyes. She lifted one perfectly manicured finger. "I call Graham!"

"What!? No fair! You didn't even give us a chance," Amberly pouted.

"I thought you had a thing for Sawyer anyway," Tiffany said, reaching for an hors d'oeuvre.

"I do not!" Amberly protested way too loudly. "But I guess if Graham is out—I mean, if I *have* to . . ."

I glanced over my shoulder at Amberly, whose blush was even deeper than mine. She was definitely not good enough for Sawyer. I almost wanted to warn him to be on the lookout for blond morons on the prowl, but I had faith that he could see right through her shiny veneer to the unoriginal soul inside.

"That leaves West and Gage," Kiran said, looking from Tiffany to Taylor. "What's it gonna be, ladies?"

"I am so not kissing Gage," Taylor said, lifting a palm. "I'll fight you for West if I have to, Goulbourne," she said to Tiff. "I've been doing cardio kickboxing three times a week for the last nine months. Consider yourself warned."

Tiffany shrugged one shoulder. "Whatever. I'll pity-kiss Gage."

"Pity-kiss?" Noelle said with a laugh. "I would *kill* to see his face if he heard that one."

Tiffany giggled, then hiccupped. She held her fingertips to her glossy lips for a moment and composed herself. "I know, right? But given what a he-slut he is, he's gotta at least have good technique."

Everyone laughed. Noelle snapped her compact shut and lifted her champagne glass. "All right, then. Now that we're all sorted, I'd like to make a toast."

We gathered together in a small circle, bubbling crystal flutes at the ready.

"To the best year of our lives," Noelle said. "But most of all, to Reed. May this year be free of drama, my little glass-licker."

My heart filled with giddy hope. The very idea that Noelle would dedicate the final toast of the year to me somehow made me feel as if her words were going to ring true.

"To Reed!" Tiffany cheered.

"And to no drama!" Kiran and Taylor added.

We all clinked glasses just as the sun dipped below the horizon.

PATIENCE

Upton's arms were locked around me in the back of the speedboat as we raced out to the private island locale Kiran had secured for our New Year's Eve bash. It was a surreal sight, all those small, sleek vessels tearing across the waves in the dark, leaving the lazy lights of the big island behind and careening toward the bonfire that raged on the beach up ahead. As we zoomed closer, I could hear the pounding of drums throbbing over the engines of the boats, and could just make out something undulating along the dock. I glanced at Upton in confusion and he shrugged. Even through my fear, being out on the water once again, I felt a thrill of excitement. This was definitely going to be a night to remember.

The boats pulled up to the dock one by one and I finally saw that the undulating was actually the movement of a dozen native dancers, moving in sync to the beat of a drums-only band. They danced around, laughing and shouting to each other, welcoming us onto the dock.

Upton helped me up from the boat and we shimmied out of our life vests, handing them to our captain. All along the dock, other guests did the same. Sawyer, Graham, and West had come over together, and Noelle and Dash had shared a boat. Bringing up the rear were Amberly, Tiffany, and Taylor, but it seemed as if there were already dozens of people on the island, mingling under big, white lights. As Upton tipped our captain, Kiran came striding down the dock in a short purple dress, her hair pinned back with one white orchid.

"Welcome to our very own island of paradise!" she shouted, earning whoops from the crowd. "And there's our guest of honor."

I shot Sawyer an apologetic look as Kiran moved forward and grabbed his arm. She dragged him to the front of the crowd, where he stared at his shoes, blushing uncontrollably.

"Now let's party!" Kiran cried.

As the group surged forward, I detached myself from Upton's side and made my way over to Sawyer. "I swear I'll make sure they keep the fawning to a minimum," I promised him.

"Thanks," Sawyer said under his breath.

I, of course, had my own plans. No matter how much he protested, I couldn't let his actions go by unheralded. But I wasn't going to go overboard. No skywriting or fireworks or anything. Just a simple speech later in the evening. After everyone, including Sawyer, had a chance to have a few drinks and decompress.

"Mind if I borrow my girl?" Upton said.

He grabbed my hand and tugged me away without waiting for an answer. I cast a glance over my shoulder at Sawyer and saw him still

standing there, left behind while everyone else joined the party. I
hoped he would find a way to get involved in the fun and let loose a
little bit, but in the next moment my attention was forcibly dragged
away. Up the sandy hill, on a rocky ledge overlooking the bonfire on
the beach, was a wide wood-plank dance floor where several attendees
were already dancing to the songs spun by the DJ. A thatched-roof bar
stood near the top of the dance floor, and the two bartenders behind
it were working so hard they were sweating. Up a rocky pathway to one
side of the bar was a burbling hot tub surrounded by flutes of champagne and trays of fruits and sweets. Down another pathway closer to
the beach was a plunge pool lit from below, its water glowing like an
aquamarine stone in the moonlight.

"Kiran has thought of everything," Upton said, pulling me close
to his side.

"I didn't think to bring a bathing suit," I told him.

"Perhaps you don't need one," he said slyly, nuzzling my ear.

"Okay, down, boy. How about we start with a dance?" I said,
pushing him away with a hand to the chest.

"All right then."

He pulled me onto the dance floor and held me so close I felt as if
every inch of my body was touching every inch of his. Upton was an
excellent dancer. He not only knew how to keep a beat, but he was so
confident and self-assured that when he moved his hands down my
back and over my hips it didn't feel awkward or contrived at all. It just
felt . . . incredible. I looked into his eyes as we danced. Soon I had
forgotten anyone else was there.

"Maybe we should get out of here," I murmured in his ear.

Upton smiled. "Patience," he said in an infuriatingly sexy tone. "Later I'm going to go back to the main island to make sure everything's arranged. I've hired one of the boats to take you back a bit after that. For now, let's just have a little fun."

With that, he grabbed my hand and twirled me away from him until our arms were perfectly straight. I was so startled I lost my balance and knocked into some random guy, who tripped into his date.

"Sorry!" I said with a laugh.

"No worries. It's a party," he replied in an Australian accent.

Couldn't have said it better myself. For the next hour we all hit the dance floor hard and heavy. The drinks were flowing and my friends got louder, messier, and more touchy-feely with each passing moment. I made sure to steer clear of the alcohol, though. Upton had said this was going to be a night neither of us would ever forget. I wanted to make sure I was completely present for all of it.

Soon a whole group of us was dancing together at the center of the dance floor, and I smiled when I saw Sawyer allow himself to get dragged in by Taylor and Amberly. He managed a smile as he joined us and just sort of stepped from side to side to the beat. But the more we all twirled and bounced and acted like complete morons, the more he seemed to relax. I even saw him touch Amberly's hip once when she was dancing all up in his face. So maybe he couldn't see through her shiny veneer, but whatever. It was a party. Let the boy have his fun.

During one of our brief breaks, I sidled over and jostled him with my elbow.

"You're having fun, aren't you?" I said. "Don't deny it, I can tell."

"It's not bad," he replied, leaning back against a palm tree near the edge of the dance floor. He looked me in the eye and smiled. "This might turn out to be an okay year after all."

I grinned. "Well, since you're in such a *positive* mood, I think I should get this over with," I said mischievously.

Sawyer, smart guy that he was, looked alarmed. He stood up straight as if ready to bolt. "What?"

"I know you hate the spotlight and everything, but I have to do this," I replied, grabbing his hand and pulling him toward the DJ. "You'll forgive me one day."

"Reed, what're you doing?" Sawyer asked, glancing around for an escape route. To his credit, however, he didn't struggle against my grip. I stepped up next to the DJ and waved him down to get his attention. "Can I get the mic for a second?" I asked.

"You Reed Brennan?" he asked.

"Yep," I replied. I had asked Kiran to clear it with him earlier.

He nodded and handed over a silver microphone. "S'all yours." Then he turned down the volume on the driving dance music until it was nothing but background noise. Gradually the people on the dance floor slowed their movements and looked around in confusion.

"Hi, everyone," I said, lifting my arm. "Sorry for the interruption. I just have a couple things I want to say."

Sawyer leaned in toward my ear. "I hate you," he whispered.

I just smiled at him.

"As many of you know, this isn't just a New Year's Eve party. We're also here to celebrate a friend of mine, Sawyer Hathaway, a guy who just happened to save my life a few nights ago," I said.

"Whoo! Go Sawyer!" Graham shouted.

Everyone laughed and applauded. Sawyer blushed, turning his profile to the crowd. He started to fiddle with the woven bracelets he always wore around his wrist, shifting his weight from one foot to the other.

"I'm going to make this brief, since he doesn't like the spotlight, but I just wanted everyone to hear me say . . . thank you, Sawyer." I turned to look at him. "If you hadn't jumped in the water at the exact moment you did, I wouldn't be here. I wouldn't be able to be with my friends, to experience this incredible party, to do any of the things I've got planned for my future." I looked at Upton as I said this and a new thrill of excitement shot through my core. "And I swear, I'll never do anything like this to you again, but I just thought you deserved a little toast."

I turned and lifted a champagne glass from a tray on the DJ's table. Kiran really *had* prepared for everything.

"To Sawyer, my hero!"

"To Sawyer!" the crowd shouted.

There was a lot of cheering and whooping and clapping. Sawyer managed to raise his hands to acknowledge it, even though he seemed to be melting in embarrassment on the inside. Soon the DJ turned up the music again and everyone got back to their dancing. I handed the microphone back to him and then gave my champagne glass to Sawyer.

"Here. Looks like you could use this," I said.

Sawyer downed the whole thing in one gulp. "Thanks."

"You don't actually hate me, do you?" I asked.

He smiled. "No. But you really are done now, right? No more thank-yous, no more speeches?"

"I swear," I said, crossing my heart for good measure.

"Omigod! You guys are *not* going to believe this!" Kiran cried, bursting out of the crowd. "Come on!"

She cut a weaving line through the dance floor—one that we attempted to follow as best we could without getting elbowed in the face. When we arrived on the other side we found that the rest of our crew was all lined up on the rocky ledge, staring out at the water. I squinted into the darkness, trying to see whatever it was that had caught their attention. Finally I zoned in on a lone boat, bobbing out on the waves a good distance offshore.

"What's up?" I asked.

"That's *Daniel's* boat," Noelle said, lifting a hand. "Those losers are out there spying on us!"

I laughed. "You're kidding."

"They are *so* pathetic," Taylor said.

Noelle extricated her iPhone from her clutch and turned it on.

"What're you doing?" Dash asked.

"Just wait." Noelle held the phone to her ear and cleared her throat. "Voice mail. Figures." She waited a moment, then spoke. "Are you really that pathetic that you couldn't find anything better to do on New Year's Eve than spy on us? Oh, Paige, how the mighty have fallen. Have fun wallowing in your friendlessness."

She dropped her phone back in her bag and turned to the rest of us. "Hot tub?"

The girls cheered and the guys tore off their shirts. Sawyer shrugged and followed Graham, who was running toward the hot tub in nothing but his boxers.

"Hope you've got a bra on under that dress," Tiffany said as she lifted her frock off over her head, revealing a matching—and very sexy—set of black lingerie.

Luckily, I did, but still . . . did I really want all the guys seeing me in my underwear? Especially Upton, who was supposed to see it *all* later? And Dash, who had already seen some of it on one of the most shameful nights of my life?

"It's sweet that you're so shy," Upton said in my ear, noting my hesitation. "Here."

He produced a blue T-shirt from behind his back and handed it to me. "I got it from one of the dancers just in case."

"Upton . . . thank you."

He brought his forehead to mine and our noses touched. "Like I really want any of these gits to see my girl half naked. You are all mine."

His words sent a shiver of delight across my shoulders, down my back, and all the way into my toes.

"Yes, I am," I replied. I pulled the large T-shirt on, then shimmied out of my dress. "Now let's get in the tub."

MY PARTY

"Are you crazy? You can't go in the pool after the hot tub! The water will be freezing," Amberly complained, shivering in her pink underwear as we all made our way down the hill toward the pool a little while later. "You're supposed to do it the other way around."

"I like to live on the edge," Kiran said flatly. "Go dry off if you don't want to come."

"Actually, I think I'm going to take that advice. You lot go ahead," Upton said, pausing halfway down the hill near the dance floor. My heart skipped a beat as Tiffany and West veered around us and kept walking, their bare feet making wet prints on the wood floor. "I need to get back. Are you all right here?"

I smiled, lifting my soggy hair over my shoulder. "I'm good. How long before I join you?" I asked, stepping forward so that our knees brushed.

Upton checked his watch. "I told the guy to come round at eleven.

You don't mind the idea of celebrating the New Year alone together, do you?"

I thought of what Kiran said about how what you're wearing when the clock strikes twelve sets the tone for the whole year. Maybe if Upton and I were alone together, wearing nothing at all, it would be a good omen for our long-distance relationship. The very thought of it sent a shiver through me. He reached out to rub my arms with his palms.

"I'm okay," I said. "Just thinking about later. And no, I don't mind celebrating alone together."

Upton's smile warmed me from head to toe. He leaned in and gave me a long, lingering kiss. "I'll see you soon."

Then he squeezed my hand once and headed down the hill in the opposite direction, toward the dock. I laced my fingers together under my chin as I watched him go, unable to believe how lucky I was. That incredibly gorgeous, sought-after, intelligent, worldly guy wanted to be with me. Just me. Tonight of all nights. New Year's Eve. He was going to leave his lifelong friends at this kick-ass party just to be with me. It was all I could do to keep from laughing out loud. Instead I turned around and traipsed down the sandy walkway to join my friends at the pool. The guys were hanging out at a couple of high-top tables, munching on finger foods while the girls were in the pool, hanging out on the steps.

"Reed, that boy is so in love with you they should write Hallmark cards about it," Kiran said as I joined them.

I eased my way into the cold water next to Noelle, unable to wipe the grin off my face.

"You so won the Upton game it's ridiculous," Tiffany added. Every year, the girls competed to see who Upton would hook up with first. It was a lovely little holiday tradition that I tried not to think about.

I tilted my head. "Well, not officially. Not *yet.*"

Noelle's eyebrows arched. "Not *yet.* Reed, you do realize that implies that you actually intend to seal the deal."

I bit my lip and dunked my head under the water. Even so I could hear them all squealing and laughing. Then Tiffany grabbed my arm and pulled me up.

"Wait, so you two are really going to do the deed?" she asked.

I nodded, finding myself unable to speak past the bubble of giddy emotion that had welled up in my throat.

"I knew it! I knew that was the special occasion Upton was planning," Noelle said, grinning in a self-satisfied way.

"*When?*" Kiran demanded, splashing me in the face. "When is this happening?"

I spit some water out of my mouth and blinked. "Okay, first, thanks for that," I said. "And tonight," I added, looking down at my T-shirt, which was floating up in the water. "That's why he just left. He's going back to his house to make sure everything's set."

"Wow. Look at you," Noelle said, nudging me with her foot. "I honestly didn't think you had it in you."

"What am I going to do, stay celibate forever?" I asked. "Thomas is gone and Josh and I are clearly over," I said, annoyed at the fact that my heart panged when I said Josh's name. "It's way past time to move on."

"Good for you," Taylor said with a nod.

"And who better to move on with than Upton Giles?" Kiran added.

"He is *so* hot," Amberly put in.

I shot her a look of death and she rolled her eyes.

"I'm just *saying*."

"Whatever. I just can't wait to get out of here and over there," I said, glancing in the direction of St. Barths. "No offense, Kiran. This party is fab, but—"

"We get it. Believe me," Kiran replied, tipping her champagne glass to me, "your party, Miss Brennan, hasn't even started."

DON'T BOTHER

I tried to ignore the lewd and immature hoots and hollers of my friends as I boarded the private boat Upton had chartered for me. It was much larger than the speedboats that had brought us out to the island, with a cabin below and steps up to the captain's perch above. The floor and all the white leather seats at the stern were completely blanketed in red and pink rose petals, and there was a folded note perched atop a white life vest.

Be safe, the note read. *I'll see you soon.*

I smiled to myself as I shrugged the vest on over my red dress, which I had changed back into after the pool, and secured the straps. It was so sweet that he'd thought of the vest, that he was taking care of me even though he wasn't there. I placed the balled-up wet T-shirt (which I'd decided to take home as a souvenir) on one of the side benches along with my purse and settled in, my heart pounding in anticipation. Soon I would be alone with Upton. I tried to imagine how it would all play out. Felt his hands on my skin and his lips over mine. I shuddered pleasantly. I couldn't wait to experience the real thing.

"All set, miss?" the boat captain called down to me. He glanced over his shoulder slightly and I saw that he had a ruddy beard and wore thick glasses.

"Yes. I'm ready," I replied.

Let's just go, go, go!

He nodded to a worker on the dock, who untied the boat from its tether. The engine sputtered to life and we pulled away lazily, making our way out to the open water. As soon as we were a few yards from the private island, the captain really opened her up, and we were flying across the open ocean, jumping waves at an alarming speed.

My heart skipped a few frightened beats and I held on to the safety rail to my right, pressing my lips together to keep myself from shouting out. I didn't want to be a big baby, but I wouldn't have imagined that a boat this large could actually move so fast. Or that it *should*. But if Upton hired this guy, I was sure he knew what he was doing. Besides, the faster we traveled, the sooner I would get to Upton's house. The sooner I would be in Upton's arms.

We jumped a large wave and the boat slammed back down into the water as if it were concrete. Every bone in my body was jarred and I closed my eyes for a second, trying to compose myself. If Noelle were here, she would definitely say something. Tell the guy to slow down. He was, after all, on Upton's payroll. Wouldn't he have to listen to Upton's guest?

Just do it, Reed. Stick up for yourself.

I opened my eyes and looked at St. Barths off the starboard side. My heart all but stopped. The island wasn't there. I glanced around, disoriented, and saw that the main island and all its sparkling lights were now behind us, the private island off in the distance to my right. We had completely turned around, headed in the darkness out to the wide-open water.

My heart vaulted into my throat. If there was one place I didn't want to be, it was the open ocean. What was wrong with this guy? Was he drunk? Had he passed out at the wheel or something?

I forced my terror to the back of my mind and pushed myself to my feet. Still clinging to the handrail, I took a shaky step forward, glad, at least, that I had worn low heels instead of the stilettos Kiran had wanted me to. The problem of course, was that the captain was standing up on a platform above me. The only way to get to him would be to climb one of the two steep sets of wet stairs on either side of the cabin. The very idea made my stomach turn like I'd just gotten off a badly constructed carnival ride.

"Excuse me!" I shouted as loud as I could. The captain didn't flinch. Didn't move. Didn't acknowledge that he had heard me. He probably hadn't, what with the roaring of the engine and the slapping of the boat against the water. "Excuse me! Hey!" I reached out for the safety rail at the bottom of the stairs and placed my trembling foot on the bottom step. "We're going the wrong way! The island is over the—"

My words were suddenly cut off as a bandana was flung over my head from behind and crammed into my mouth. I tried to scream, but the gag was already tied tightly. It shoved my tongue into my throat, and I started to choke. As I fought for breath, I was yanked backward off my feet and my butt slammed into the floor. Instinctively, I reached up to try to claw at my attacker, but my arms were quickly pinned behind my back and tied together with rough twine. I winced in pain as the rope cut my skin. My eyes rolled wildly around, begging the captain to look behind him, to see what was happening, to help me. But even as my feet pounded the floor, he didn't move. I tried to squirm forward using my feet and glutes, but the guy grabbed my hair and yanked me back. The pain was sudden and unexpected and excruciating. Then he placed his hand over my forehead and slammed the back of my skull into the floor, which was still covered in Upton's rose petals.

"Don't bother, bitch," he spat, his voice gruff, his face turned away from me.

I forced myself to breathe through my nose, but my panic was so great, I was barely able to take in any air. Pain radiated throughout my skull. Tears stung my eyes and coursed down my face, but I forced myself to stare at my attacker. Tried to commit any details I could to memory. He wore dark glasses that all but covered his face, and had a thick beard just like the captain, but this one was dark and wiry.

It was the last thing I saw before my eyes were blindfolded, and I was truly powerless.

PRANK

About two seconds later, he threw me down the stairs like a sack of dirty laundry. My knees hit the ground first and I careened forward, slamming the side of my head against something sharp. I shouted out in pain and rolled over onto my back, my shoulder muscles straining as I pinned my already tethered arms underneath my weight. I struggled to sit up, the side of my head throbbing angrily, and felt blood trickling down behind my ear. The boat took a sudden turn and I slid across the floor, my entire body slamming into the wall.

That was when I really started to cry. Tears soaked my blindfold and my nose quickly stuffed itself with mucus. Suddenly, I couldn't breathe to save my life. I gasped past the gag and my lungs constricted over and over and over again. I was going to die. I was going to cry myself to death.

Get control, Reed. Calm down. Just. Calm. Down.

Coughing a few times and sucking in a few more breaths, I

managed to clear my nasal passages. Then I sat for what felt like an eternity, breathing in and out, in and out, until my heart rate calmed to a relatively normal state.

Normal for someone who was suffering from multiple head traumas, who couldn't see and couldn't move, who was being kidnapped off the coast of a remote Caribbean island at a time when no one would notice she was missing for at least an hour.

I was completely screwed.

Overhead, I heard the pounding of footsteps and shouting voices. Obviously, my attacker and the captain of the boat were in on this together. So even if I'd gotten Red Beard's attention, he wouldn't have been any help to me. As I thought back to what little I'd seen of their faces, I started to realize that the beards were obviously fake. The glasses clearly a misdirect. So who the hell were these people? Was Daniel one of them? It made sense. Daniel hated Upton, and Paige hated me. Maybe the two of them had decided to kill two birds with one stone. Devastate Upton by getting rid of me. Maybe even send him crying into Paige's arms. Was that why they had been hovering out there in their boat, watching the party? Were they waiting for Upton to leave so that they could put their plan into action?

My heart seized with a sudden realization. The guy who had been arrested for shoving me off the boat had been on the Ryan family's payroll. Had Daniel and Paige orchestrated that too? Had they paid him off? Promised to take care of his family if he didn't say anything to the police about them? It all made sense. The twins could have been behind every one of my near misses. I had been on their estate when the horse took off and almost rode me off a cliff. One of them could have hidden in the bushes and spooked her. I had been on Daniel's Jet Ski when it malfunctioned and almost killed me. He definitely could have rigged that. And I had been on their family's boat when someone in their family's employ had shoved me over the rail and left me for dead. Plus both Sawyer and Taylor had noticed the two of them taking off right around the time I'd gone over.

It all made sense.

But knowing this didn't make me feel any better. If anything, I was even more terrified. They had been trying to kill me for days. And now they had me out in the middle of nowhere with no one looking for me. If I was late to meet Upton, he'd probably think I wasn't done partying yet. And no one on the private island would realize I was missing until tomorrow morning.

I felt my eyes start to well up again and forced the tears down. If I was going to survive this, I was going to have to be strong. Maybe they weren't out to kill me. Maybe they were just messing with me. Playing a prank. Teaching me a lesson. God, I hoped that was true.

The boat took another sharp turn and I skidded across the floor again, falling onto my side as my leg slammed into the opposite wall. I shouted out in pain, but it came out as a pathetic gargle thanks to my gag. A few seconds later, the boat jolted and the bottom scraped across rocks or sand. Whatever it was, wherever we were, we'd run ashore.

There was more shouting. I sat up straight and tilted my ear toward the ceiling, trying to make it out. The two voices were definitely male, but I couldn't tell if one belonged to Daniel. Maybe Paige and the other girls were in on the planning of this insanity but just didn't want to mess up their manicures by doing any of the dirty work. Whoever the men were, I couldn't make out their words. Footsteps pounded across the deck and I heard something bang against the side wall of the cabin. They were still talking as the hatch overhead opened, letting cool night air pour over my semi-clothed body. The only words I heard were the tail end of a sentence. Words that stopped me cold.

". . . then find somewhere to dump the body."

This was no prank. These men were going to kill me.

PRETTY-BOY BILLIONAIRE

"Please. Please, please, please, please, please."

I tried to beg, but the gag in my mouth distorted the words. I tripped forward across the deck as they dragged me by one arm. My head throbbed in several places and my knees and thighs were sore with the beginnings of nasty bruises. I heard a splash. Someone shoved me from behind and my feet hit the water. I started to fall forward, but the second guy yanked me to my feet and pushed his hand into the small of my back. I fumbled ahead, my feet unsteady as I navigated the shallow incline toward the shore. Soon, my toes hit dry sand. The moment they did I was shoved again, and fell face-first into the sand.

My captors—my executioners—laughed. Rage surged through me like white-hot fire. One of them tugged at the knot on my gag and it fell free. I coughed as I rolled over, still blindfolded. There was no light coming through the slits at the top and bottom of the black scarf that was tied over my eyes. Definitely still night. Apparently, we hadn't been on the water for very long.

I felt proud of myself for noticing these things, for trying to assess my situation, even though I was terrified for my life.

"Any last words?" one of them asked.

I swallowed hard. I was pretty sure it was Red Beard speaking. At least it sounded like the boat captain's voice. But now I felt a shiver of recognition. I swore I had heard that voice before. But where? I thought back to every man I had met on the island and couldn't place it. Could it be Daniel disguising his voice?

"Please don't kill me," I blubbered as I was dragged to my feet again. I hated that I couldn't even see them. That they wouldn't even look me in the eye. That I was standing on some beach somewhere and I didn't even know what it looked like. What the place of my death looked like. "Please. You don't have to do this."

"God, just shut her up," one of them whispered. "Enough already."

I pulled in a shaky breath. "Why are you—"

My words died in my throat. Something hard had just been pressed into the back of my skull. I heard the click as the gun's hammer was cocked.

"No!" I screamed at the top of my lungs, releasing every ounce of my soul into the air. Fear coursed through my body like cold shock waves. I trembled, more terrified than I had been that night on the roof of Billings with Ariana. More terrified than I'd felt looking down the barrel of Sabine's gun. At least then I had known where I was, had had the benefit of sight. Had known there were people around who could help me. But now, I was alone. Completely blind, completely helpless.

Images flitted rapid-fire through my mind. Josh, Thomas, Billings, Noelle, my home in Croton, my parents, my brother, my dog, my first bike, my first soccer uniform, my turtle—God, I'd forgotten I ever had a turtle—my dolls, my baby blanket, my room.

And Upton. Upton, Upton, Upton waiting for me in his bedroom on St. Barths. The bottle of wine, the look of anticipation on his face. My heart felt as if it was being shredded by a raging lion as I thought of him.

"I have a rich boyfriend!" I shouted, sounding like a pathetic crazy. "He'll pay you. He'll pay you anything. Please just don't shoot me!"

For the first time, my captors were completely silent. My heart swelled with hope. Clearly I had gotten their attention.

But then they laughed.

"That's not going to work," one of them said. This one, I realized, hadn't spoken until now. His English was clipped. As if he was concentrating on his words. It must have been the second man. The one who had gagged me and thrown me around the boat. "You see, we are already being paid to kill you."

The air rushed out of my lungs. "What?" I breathed.

"I don't know what you did, little girl, but you've definitely pissed off some very important people," Red Beard said.

People. Plural. Daniel and Paige. It *had* to be them. That family was just crazy enough to spawn a plan like this. Just rich enough to have the money to do it. But why? Why go to all this trouble to get rid of me?

In a week I was going to be back at Easton and they'd never have to see me again. The gun pressed deeper into my skull.

"Wait! But Upton . . . he's a billionaire. Trust me, whatever you're being paid, he'll double it." I took a deep breath as the pressure of the gun lessened. "Think about it for a second. You can walk away with twice the money and no blood on your hands."

The gun was lowered and they shoved me to my knees. For a second I thought they were just going to pull the trigger and I pressed my eyes closed under my blindfold. I couldn't breathe. My whole body involuntarily flinched over and over and over again, thinking each second was my last on earth. Waiting for the shot was torture, pure and simple. My teeth clenched together, and every inch of my body shook.

But then the gun was lowered, and I felt them walk away. Felt their eerie, looming presence subside. Their voices carried to me on the wind in snippets as they discussed my offer.

"That kid . . . would never . . ."

I twisted my hands around, trying to loosen the twine that bound my wrists together. The rope only cut deeper into my flesh. I bit my lip to muffle my cry and kept twisting. This pain was preferable to getting shot.

". . . say we just get it over . . ."

Slowly, I sat down on my butt and swung my legs around in the sand so my feet were in front of me.

". . . is true, we could just get . . ."

Holding my breath, I pushed myself up to standing, sidestepping a bit for balance.

"... no idea what she's talking about ..."

I took a step forward, not knowing what the hell I would find up ahead, but knowing it had to be better than what I had here.

"... but that fa— Hey!"

My heart seized at the sound of his shout. Within two seconds the gun was pressed into my skull again, right against one of my many fresh wounds. The pain was so sharp I choked out a cry.

"Where the hell do you think you're going?" Mr. Stilted English spat.

"Please! Please, don't," I cried.

"Jesus. If we're going to do this let's just do it," Red Beard said.

"Fine."

I waited for the gun to go off. Wondered if I would have time to feel the pain.

And then he released me.

"We're gonna go talk to that pretty-boy billionaire of yours," Red Beard said. "Good luck not freezing to death out here."

I heard them moving off through the sand and relief rushed through me. All my emotions welled to the surface and I started to cry. Bawl, actually, but I no longer cared. I just let it all out. I was alive. That was all that mattered. For the moment, I was alive.

The boat's engine roared to life. I was still crying when it faded to nothing in the distance. They were going to talk to Upton. Upton was going to save me.

Everything was going to be all right.

CALL FOR HELP

Or not.

As soon as the boat's engine was out of earshot, I realized the hopelessness of the situation. I wasn't dead. That was something. But I *was* standing on the middle of a beach, blindfolded, with my hands tied behind my back. It was the middle of the night and I was wearing only a skimpy minidress, with nothing to protect me from the cold breeze that was kicking up off the water. I assumed the island was deserted, which meant no one was about to stumble upon me and help me. But there could be animals. Huge, scary animals that liked to tear apart human flesh.

Once again, my heart started to pound.

"Okay . . . okay . . . all you've got to do is keep yourself alive until Upton pays those guys off," I said to myself, my chest heaving up and down with my panicked breathing. But my brain wouldn't stop. How far was I from St. Barths? How long would it take them to get there, to find him, to do the deal? I tilted my head back, trying to see something, anything, through the slit of an opening at the bottom of the blindfold. All I could see were my bare feet. My shoes were gone. Not that they were exactly survival gear, but still. It would have been nice to have them. I wondered when they had fallen off. In the boat? In the water? I couldn't remember. I hadn't exactly been thinking about footwear while those guys were talking about dumping my body.

The wind kicked up and I took a deep breath. First things first. I had to get this blindfold off so I could assess my situation. Find shelter. I sat down carefully, my arms still tethered behind my back, and lay back in the cool sand. Digging my head back as hard as I could into the ground, I squirmed forward down the beach, trying to dislodge the blindfold. The knot edged up a little bit. My heart leapt with hope and I squirmed some more. And some more. The knot edged up ever so slightly again, this time hitting the bruise left when Mr. Stilted English had slammed my head into the floor. Hatred and anger surged through me and I squirmed even harder. By the time I felt the knot moving up the back of my skull again, I was sweating from exertion.

But at least I wasn't cold anymore.

Finally, with one last push, the blindfold came free. Yes! Relief rushed through me. I sat up and looked around. Thanks to the ever-present blanket of stars, and a nice, fat moon, the night wasn't pitch-black. I could see that the beach was wide and white, reaching up to a thick forest of vegetation behind me. To my left was a long, flat rocky ledge stretching out into the water. To my right, nothing but sand stretching on for what seemed like miles. Out in the ocean . . .

nothing. No sign of St. Barths or Kiran's party island or any boats of any kind. There was nothing but water as far as I could see.

All I had was my blindfold, and the bandana they had used as a gag, which was lying in the sand a few feet up the beach. No food. No water. No blanket. No tent. Nothing, nothing, nothing.

Hopelessness started to cave in on me like a thousand tons of rocks. Where was I supposed to go? Into the trees where animals probably lived? It wasn't like I could sit out here all night on the cold beach in the wind. I would, as Red Beard implied, freeze to death.

Could that happen in one night? Would Upton sail out here to rescue me only to find my cold, dead body?

No. I was being ridiculous. This was the Caribbean. Sure the nights were cool, but not freezing. And there had to be something I could do. I shoved myself to my feet, ready to check out the tree line, and saw something out of the corner of my eye. Something tossed into the sand near the edge of the water. My heart leapt with hope and I ran for the water's edge. It was my purse, my still-wet T-shirt, and one of my shoes. The men must have thrown my things there, intending to bury them with me or something. Get rid of the evidence. But the stupid morons hadn't realized something. My phone was in that purse!

I dropped to my knees and leaned forward, grabbing at the clutch with my teeth. I only succeeded in pushing it farther away. If these things got any closer to the water, the tide was going to come in and sweep it out to sea. Cursing under my breath, I got up again and kicked all of it up the beach, working my way up until I was a few feet away from the forest's edge.

"Okay. How the hell do I get at my phone?" I said through my teeth.

I looked down at my bare feet. It was worth a shot. Sitting my butt down on the cold sand, I managed to pull the purse toward me by gripping it between my feet. Then I held it down with the sole of one foot while nudging the toes of my other foot under the flap. The second it opened, it flapped closed again, the magnetic closure working against me.

"Dammit!" I cried, frustrated tears stinging my eyes.

This was ridiculous. I needed my hands. Even if I got the damn phone out of there, it was going to be impossible to work the touch screen with my sandy toes. I shoved myself to my knees, then my feet, and walked toward the flat rock. There had to be something there I could use. Something sharp to cut the twine, or something I could use as a wedge to shimmy the coil from my wrists. I walked all the way around the base of the rock. There were plenty of stones, but all of them had been smoothed out by the pounding surf. The desperation was just starting to fill my chest again, when I saw a large patch of white clinging to the black rock. I moved closer to inspect it and saw that it was a colony of rough barnacles, porous and scaly, almost like a pumice stone.

My jaw clenched. It would take hours to break through the twine this way. But it was the only hope I had.

I turned around, backed my hands into the barnacles, and started to move my arms up and down. The barnacles snagged my skin and I winced in pain. I leaned forward slightly, trying to keep my arms away from the sharp surface as much as possible, and kept going. Up, down, up, down, up, down. I kept catching my skin, and each time it stung even worse, but I just gritted my teeth and kept working. At times it felt as if the twine was loosening, but then I'd try to pull my hands apart and nothing would happen.

After what felt like an eternity, I stepped away from the rock, panting with exertion and exhaustion and fear and pain, and pulled as hard as I could. My wrists felt as if they were being slit open with a paring knife. I shouted against the pain and strained even harder. Harder, harder, until I couldn't take it anymore.

Nothing happened.

That was when I let out a scream that scared a dozen birds from one of the trees at the edge of the forest. My heart constricted at the reminder that I was not alone, and I went back to work.

Gritting my teeth, I told myself that the pain wasn't there. I moved my shoulders up and down, tearing my wrists apart, and simply took it. There was no other option. I needed my hands, and this was the only way to free them. Sweat popped up along my lip, across my brow, under my arms. My wrists burned. I clenched my jaw tighter and kept going.

Two minutes later, the rope fell into the shallow water at my feet. I was free. *Yes, yes, yes, yes, yes!*

I whipped my arms around to inspect them. There were nasty, bloody cuts around my wrists and scrapes all up and down my forearms. The wounds stung in the cold night air, but the pain was nothing. I was free.

I turned around and sprinted for my phone. Falling to my knees in front of my clutch, I ripped it open and dumped its contents onto the ground. My heart fell to my toes. My phone was not there.

"No! No! No!" I shouted, moving aside the lip gloss, the compact, the Tic Tacs. As if an iPhone could be hiding beneath any of this stuff. Of course it wasn't there. The men had been smart enough, at least, to take that with them. There would be no calling for help. No relief of friendly voices. Nothing to do but wait.

I lifted my shredded wrists and took in a long, broken breath. All that work, all that pain, all this blood . . . for nothing.

I turned around to face the ocean, curled my knees up under my chin, rested my face between them, and cried.

NO STOPPING HER

The sun streamed down from above, warming my face as I looked out over the sparkling blue Caribbean Sea. I leaned against the cool, metal guardrail in my little red dress, feeling the wind in my face as the boat pushed forward through the waves. The water curled against the bow, burbling happily into white foam. I tipped my head back, my hair ticking the bare skin on my back. I was free. Free and totally at peace. Nothing could touch me now.

"You are the most beautiful girl I've ever seen."

I turned and smiled at Thomas Pearson as he stepped up to the rail next to me. He was wearing a white T-shirt and jeans and looked perfectly gorgeous. Untouched. Handsome and tan and young and alive. Behind him, the sun was descending toward the horizon at a rapid pace, but it didn't bother me. Thomas was here. His hand on the small of my back. His touch was firm and warm. I leaned my head on his shoulder and breathed in the musky, clean scent of him.

"I love you, Reed. You're the only girl I ever loved."

"I know," I told him, lifting my head. "You told me."

Thomas smiled, then looked at something over my shoulder. "Hey, man."

I turned around. It was Josh. His curly hair danced in the wind and he was wearing that sweater I loved so much. The green one with the high neck that brought out his eyes. It was dusk now, the sky a rich purple, and stars were beginning to appear overhead.

"Hey," Josh said. He leaned in and touched his lips to mine. I melted all over.

"You love me too," I told him.

"Of course I do," he said, his hand sliding up under my hair. "I just had to do what was right. You know that."

"She does. She's fine," Upton said, joining us. He slid between me and Thomas, and Thomas stepped back with a laugh, raising his hands in surrender. "I'll take care of her," Upton told them. "Don't worry."

Upton slipped his hand into mine, our fingers entwined. We looked up at the now dark sky, where a blanket of stars twinkled and winked like huge, fat diamonds.

"I want one," I said.

"I'll get it for you," Upton offered with a smile.

"No. It's okay. I've got it."

I climbed up on the railing, my feet completely steady, and reached as high as I could. There was one star hanging impossibly low, just above my head, just at the edge of my grasp. I stood on my toes—for some reason I was wearing only one shoe—and stretched my fingers, reaching . . . reaching . . . reaching. . . .

"Reed, what're you doing?" Thomas asked, an amused smile playing on his lips.

"Don't. You're going to fall," Upton warned.

"Don't bother, man," Josh said, slapping Upton on the back. "There's no stopping her when she gets like this."

I looked down at them with a smile, ready to scold them for talking about me as if I wasn't there, and all of a sudden, my feet slipped. My heart swooped into my throat. I reached out, grappling for something, anything, to grab on to, but there was nothing. A scream of terror escaped my lips as I fell. Plunged right past the guardrail and the three smiling loves of my life. And that was when I saw it. The hooded figure. It hovered just behind them, out of their sight, marking my progress as I fell.

My heart seized with fear. Whoever it was, they were going to make sure they succeeded this time. They were going to make absolutely sure I never saw daylight again.

"Upton! Turn around!" I shouted. "He's right there!"

But then I hit the water, and the salty, roiling ocean closed over my face.

I couldn't breathe. I clawed and kicked and strained, but the water felt like pudding. It slowed my progress. Tired my muscles. It took everything I had to shove my way to the surface. When I finally got there, I gasped in a breath, ready to scream, but Upton, Josh, and Thomas were gone. The hooded figure stood alone at the back of the boat now, staring down at me as the vessel moved steadily away from me. If I could just figure out who it was. If I could just see its face . . .

And then, the figure moved. Slim white hands lifted the hood away and long blond hair streamed out over the ocean in the wind. My blood stopped cold.

It was Ariana. She was still trying to kill me. After all this time, she hadn't given up. Her lips were set in a cold, thin smile, her light blue eyes like ice as she gazed down at me.

I was just about to let out a shout when something cold and slimy closed around my ankle and yanked me under. I opened my mouth and it filled with frigid, salty water. My lungs flooded. My heart exploded. And all the while Ariana smiled down at me. Down . . . down . . . down . . .

I gasped and sat up straight. My body shivered, my bones so frigid they were radiating cold from the inside out. I wrapped my arms around myself and held on tight, trying to abate the trembling. The sun was up, but not hot enough yet to melt away the cold. Definitely not hot enough to erase the nightmare.

Taking a deep breath, I tried to shove the images out of my mind. My pulse started to slow as my wakening mind began to accept the fact that it was all a dream. I wasn't drowning. Wasn't dead. Ariana was not here.

But neither was Upton. Or Josh. Or Thomas.

I wasn't dead. Wasn't drowning. But I was still alone. And stranded.

KARANA

My stomach grumbled. I hadn't eaten anything at the party the night before, since I'd been too excited about my night with Upton to even think about food. Lesson learned. Always eat at a party, just in case you're going to be kidnapped and left for dead.

I forced a laugh, pretending my situation wasn't as dire as I knew it was, and pushed myself to my feet. Without my phone and with no watch to speak of, I had no idea what time it was, but the sun was hanging low over the horizon, so it had to be early. I wondered if there was anything to eat on this island. Any fruit-bearing trees or shrubs. If there were, I was going to find them. At least it would give me something to do. A task with which to distract myself until Upton showed up with the cavalry.

Please, God, let Upton be on his way. He would pay those guys off for me, right? He loved me. Money was nothing when it came to a person's life. Especially someone you loved. Right?

Suddenly I found myself wishing we had known each other for more than a week.

But I couldn't think that way. I had to have confidence in Upton. He was going to do the right thing. He was going to come for me.

I picked up the still-wet, balled-up T-shirt and opened it up, slapping as much sand off it as I could. Then I laid it out on a flat rock in the sun to dry in case the wind kicked up later. It would be nice to have another layer of clothing. I fished my compact from my purse to check the wound on the side of my head. There was a cut above my ear and my hair was caked with dried blood. I winced at the blood and touched my fingertips to the area. It didn't hurt too badly, and it seemed as if the cut had started to heal. At least that was a good thing.

Pulling my scraggly, tangled hair back, I secured it into a low ponytail using the bandana that was formerly my gag. Then I picked up the rest of my things—my purse, my shoe, and the black strip of fabric that was once my blindfold, and stashed it all behind a rock near the tree line. I was pretty sure no one was going to come along and steal it, but at least it would be safe from the elements. I was about to set off on my search when, on second thought, I took the shoe and the blindfold with me. If I found fresh water I could clean up my cut with the bandana. And if I needed to crack open a coconut or something I could use the heel of the shoe.

Did they even have coconuts around here?

Whatever. I was impressed with myself for even thinking of it.

I took a deep breath and started to walk. I stayed on the sand but kept to the tree line, checking every new bit of vegetation I found for any kind of apple, berry, or similar sustenance. There seemed to be nothing but leaves. Big, fat fronds and tiny curved buds and scaly-looking yellow things. But all leaves. No fruit anywhere. As I walked, the beach grew slimmer and slimmer, the waves crashing closer to my feet. There was a big outcropping of rocks up ahead, stretching right from the water all the way up to the trees. If I was going to get past it, I would have to climb over. I paused and stood on my toes, trying to see over to the other side, but the wall of rock was just a bit taller than I was. I looked back to my camp. The light blue shirt was the only speck of color on the beach and it was just that—a speck. I had already walked pretty far. I might as well see what this island was all about. Who knew? Maybe on the other side of this rock wall there was a happening Club Med with an open bar and all-you-can-eat barbecue.

My stomach grumbled again. I tied the blindfold around my wrist, gripped my shoe between my teeth, and started to climb. The rocks were wet and slippery, but there were plenty of ledges and cracks to help me on my way. I slipped only once, slamming my elbow into a sharp edge, but the resulting throbbing didn't even slow me down. I was getting used to pain and bruises. At the top, I pressed my knees into the cold surface and shoved myself to my feet.

There was no Club Med. And this wasn't just a rock wall. It was a huge expanse of rocky terrain that made up the entire shoreline as far as the eye could see. The waves crashed against the uneven ledge, sending angry spray up toward the sky. A very unfriendly omen. There was no point in moving forward. If I was going to find food or shelter, I was going to have to double back and try the other direction.

Feeling defeated, I turned to make the slow climb back down to the beach. That was when I saw a whole mess of driftwood. It was floating in a wide puddle that had formed in an indentation atop the rock. The wood pieces were smooth and perfectly formed, like they were planks from a doomed skiff or rowboat. I walked over and picked one up. The edges were sharp, but the top and bottom were smooth as silk. I had no idea what I might use it for, but it seemed like it could come in handy.

I dragged the plank to the edge of the rocky steppe, threw it to the sand along with my shoe, then climbed down after it.

On the way back to my little stretch of beach, I walked along the water's edge. The tide tossed hundreds of shells being tossed forward and back. Every now and then I paused to pick one up and inspect it, then flung it out into the water. I thought of Sawyer and wondered if he and the rest of my friends knew what was going on. Had the kidnappers found Upton? If they had, had he alerted everyone else, or was he trying to keep the whole thing quiet?

Noelle might not be up for another few hours. How long would it be before she realized I was missing and not just squirreled away with Upton somewhere on a romantic rendezvous? Suddenly I remembered her toast from the evening before. How she'd wished I'd have a drama-free year. Apparently that wish was not going to come true.

I felt tears start to well up in my eyes and I swallowed them back. Shells skittered into my feet and ankles as the water rolled in, then skittered away again. I saw a big flat white shell start to dance its way, end over end, out into the water. When it was thrust back again, I bent down and grabbed it.

One of my favorite books in middle school was *Island of the Blue Dolphins*. In it, an Indian girl named Karana marked her time on a deserted island using a shell and a smooth plank of wood. Maybe that was why I had grabbed this piece of driftwood that was now tucked under my arm. Maybe my subconscious had been thinking about Karana.

I clutched the shell and walked a little ways up the beach. Then I sat down in the sand, took a deep breath, and cut a long, white line into the wood. One morning. My first morning on the island. Hopefully it would be my last.

In a good way, of course.

I sat back on my elbows and watched the water, looking for Upton's sailboat or Noelle's father's cruiser or anything, really. Anything that could save me. When I got off this island and found out who had paid those men to kill me, I was going to make sure they rotted in hell. I would tell my story five thousand times, testify in court, do whatever the hell I had to do to ensure they were locked up for a long, long time. Forever wouldn't be long enough.

And then I was going to make sure I never took anything for granted again. I was going to graduate from Easton with the highest honors and go to Harvard. I was going to kick ass in college and have fun with friends and take risks and say yes to everything. Except vacations to the Caribbean. That ship had definitely sailed.

And I was going to eat. All the time. I was going to get big and fat and be full, full, full all the time. I imagined what my first meal back on St. Barths would be. The burgers at Shutters were pretty damn good. That was what I wanted. A burger and fries and a chocolate milk shake. Maybe ten of them.

My stomach growled angrily and I put my hand over my abdomen as if I could somehow soothe it.

Please, just let Upton come for me today, I thought, looking down at the white line in the plank. Please. I just want to go home.

But he didn't come. No one did.

MEAT EATER

The rain came out of nowhere. At least I think it did. I was sleeping on the beach, curled up in a ball at the edge of the tree line, when suddenly I was being pelted with ten thousand zinging, stinging drops of ice-cold water. I woke up, gathered my things in my arms, and stumbled into the jungle in a state of semiconscious, panicked confusion.

The sky was gray, meaning it was morning. My third morning. When I found someplace to settle, I was going to have to carve another line in my plank of wood. *If* I found someplace to settle. Cold water slithered down my back, and I looked around the forest for some kind of shelter. The drops were less fierce under the cover of the trees, but I was still getting soaked. I took a few tentative steps forward, my bare feet crunching over sand and leaves and twigs. The underbrush was so thick and scraggly that I couldn't even see my feet. It would be so easy to step on something sharp—a shell or a rock. Or worse, some kind of odd, poisonous bug or snake or spider. The thought sent dread slicing through me and suddenly I was afraid to move. I stood there for a moment, listening to the sound of the driving rain hitting the waxy leaves, wondering what kind of animals might be watching me at this very moment. Might be sizing me up for their breakfast.

I heard a rustle and whirled around. A branch behind me swayed as if something had just leapt off of it. My heart catapulted to my throat. Another rustle sounded, this time to my left. I turned, but didn't see anything. Something skittered across my foot.

I yelped in terror and jumped about three feet in the air.

Thunder rumbled overhead and the rain came down even harder. I stared helplessly at the trees, tears welling in my eyes. I had two choices. Find a tree to hide out under, or go back out to the beach and be pounded by the elements.

I took a deep breath.

"You're just imagining things," I told myself, rounding my shoulders and adjusting my meager belongings in my arms. What was it my father had always told me when I was little and terrified by the spiders in our basement?

"They're more afraid of you than you are of them."

Right. Anything that was living on this little island was going to be afraid of me. After all, it was pretty clear they didn't get a lot of human visitors around here. To them I'd be a giant, freakish monster. Hopefully.

There was a blinding flash of lightning followed by a crack of thunder so fierce the ground shook. Just like that, I was on the move.

A few minutes of careful hiking and I came to a small, circular patch of land filled with soft, knee-high plants. The area was surrounded by large trees. One of them had thick, heavily vegetated branches, and the ground beneath it looked dry compared to the mud in which my bare feet were now mired. I ducked under the branches and sat down with my back against the trunk, then let out a breath I hadn't realized I was holding. It was perfectly dry under the canopy of branches. I wrapped my arms around my shivering self and smiled slightly.

See? I could do this. I could survive.

I lay the plank of wood down on the dirt in front of me. Then I removed my shell from my sopping wet silk clutch.

"I can't believe this," I said aloud. "Three mornings. Why am I still here?"

Three mornings without food. Without water. Without anyone to talk to. How much longer could I do this?

"Stop it," I told myself. "Stop it, now."

I was not going to start a pity party now. I had just found myself a dry place to wait out the storm. That had to count for something. I dug the shell into the plank and made a third line. I should be proud of the fact that I had made it through the last few days. Proud that I was still here to *draw* these lines. Proud that I—

I heard another rustle. My heart stopped beating. I squinted past the branches of my tree into the gray forest. A crunch. A loud *series* of crunches. Holy crap. The leaves on the plants outside my tree were moving. Something was out there. Hidden beneath the camouflaging leaves of the plant life. And it was coming this way.

I dropped the shell and picked up the plank of wood. Glancing around, I wondered if I should run. But if I did, would it chase me? One glance back at the vegetation and I realized it was too late. The thing was coming on fast, cutting a direct path through the underbrush, right for me. I pressed my back into the rough bark of the tree, pulled my knees up as close to my body as they could get, and wielded the plank like a baseball bat.

I was just going to have to defend myself.

It was three feet away.

Please just don't let it have sharp teeth.

Two feet.

I don't think I can do this.

One.

I wanted to close my eyes, but knew I couldn't. I had to defend myself; there was no one else here to do it.

The underbrush stopped moving. There was a prolonged moment of complete stillness, save for the rain pounding overhead. Maybe I had imagined it all. Maybe there was nothing there. My muscles started to relax.

And then, something flung itself at my feet.

I screamed at the top of my lungs, jumping up and slamming the top of my head into a tree limb. I was going to die. This thing was going to attack me.

I looked down at the ground, my head throbbing angrily, and froze. Looking up at me was a yellowish-green lizard, about the size of a kitten. It stared at me inquisitively with one eye, its head turned to the side. Its little pink tongue flicked out, then back, then out, then back.

It was actually kind of cute.

But that didn't mean it wasn't vicious. Or poisonous. Or even meat eating.

"Um, hi," I said quietly. "Sorry if I disturbed you, but . . . could you go away now?"

The lizard thing turned its head, looked at me with its other eye for a moment, then skittered off into the forest.

Ever so slowly I sank back down to the ground, my nerves still trembling. I placed my head between my knees, curled my shoulders forward, and laughed. I laughed for what felt like ten minutes. Laughed until my sides hurt and tears were streaming down my face. It was a great release. A necessary release. And when I was done, I was exhausted.

I crossed my arms atop my knees, rested my cheek on them, and looked down at the three white lines on my plank.

"Upton, you'd better show up today," I said under my breath. "You get one more day. After that, we're going to have to have some serious conversations about where this relationship is headed."

DONE

Five lines. Five pretty white lines on a dark piece of wood. One, two, three, four, five. Five mornings with no food. Five mornings with no shelter. Five mornings with no sign of Upton Giles, the guy who claimed he loved me.

I had really thought Upton was going to save me. I figured he'd pay the guys off, find out where I was, and swoop in to rescue me. Obviously, that hadn't happened. So what *had* happened, exactly? Would I ever know? Was I going to die on this stupid fruitless, foodless, waterless island never knowing why?

God, I had turned into a whiner. I was such a whiner I was starting to annoy myself. But then, I had no one else to talk to. And really, if you can't whine in a situation like this, when *can* you whine?

Why hadn't I gotten on that commercial flight to Atlanta? Why hadn't I followed my instincts and fled? Because Noelle and Upton had convinced me to stay. I had allowed two people who clearly didn't give two shits about me to keep me here. Here, where I was clearly going to die.

Two shits. That was a funny expression.

The bandana that was formerly my gag was covering my head, two corners tied under my chin to secure it. It was morning, so I had removed the T-shirt that had been serving as a meager blanket at night, and sat at the edge of the tree line in my now tattered and muddy red dress. Last night it had rained again and I had ventured back the woods, looking for my tree, but I hadn't been able to find it. Instead I had spent way too much time wandering hopelessly in circles, tipping fat leaves toward my lips to drink the tiny, tiny puddles of water that had formed there. My stomach had reacted with anger. Obviously, it had assumed something better was coming, not just a few teaspoons of water. I had retched it all up moments later, my knees pressed into the cold, wet earth, my hands braced on a fallen log.

Not my finest moment.

But then, none of the moments on this island had been. Not the hours I had spent trying to use my compact mirror to light a fire, which had never worked. Not the spectacular fall I had taken from the rock ledge while trying to spear those teeny-tiny fish with a branch. Not the many, many, many nervous breakdowns I'd had, crying out for Upton, for my parents, for Josh, for anyone. There was a point last night, when the rain had been pounding down around me and I had been shivering uncontrollably under the darkened branches of a twisted, nightmarish tree that gave less than zero shelter, when I had even wished the kidnappers would come back.

Because clearly I was going to die here. And if they came back, it would at least be quick.

Where were they? Maybe Upton had refused to pay. Maybe they had gone to the person who had hired them, told whoever it was that I was already dead, taken their money and gone. Why not? I was as good as dead. This way, they didn't have to waste all that gas, not to mention the bullet it would take, to finish the job.

I looked down at my arms, raging red with sunburn, and pressed my lips together against the onslaught of horrifying emotions. Above all, I was disappointed in myself. I had always thought I was a strong person. A survivor. But as it turned out, I was helpless—and hopeless. I hadn't been able to make fire. Hadn't been able to find shelter. Hadn't eaten a thing in five days. In books and movies, when people were thrown into this situation, they always rose to the occasion. They fashioned axes out of sharp rocks and homes out of tree limbs and palm fronds. They learned to catch fish, clean them, cook them, and eat them. They even found ways to entertain themselves, tossing rocks or chasing crabs or exploring caves.

But I was bored. Bored, tired, scared, starving, weak, stupid, useless, friendless, loveless, sunburned, dirty, and done.

I stared at the pile of driftwood I had built for the fire I had been so certain I was going to start. The wood was gnarly and bleached white from the sun. If I looked at it just so, it could have been a pile of bones.

That was what I was going to look like when—if—anyone ever found me.

One big pile of bleached white bones.

WATCHING

Six white lines. Six. Yesterday I had assumed I would never see six white lines. Had assumed I'd be dead before that could happen.

But I woke up this morning. Not dead.

Weird.

It was another beautiful, sunny day in the Caribbean. Not a cloud in sight. Somewhere people were reveling in this fact. They'd picked a good week for vacation, all right! But not me. I would have given up a limb for a cloudy day. My skin was peeling off in long strips. As much as I tried to stay in the shade, it was freezing the moment I stepped—or crawled, usually—from the beach into the tree line. Unbearably so. Freezing inside, scorching out. There was no in between. And so, I was burned. My lips were chapped and blistered. My throat as dry as the sand under my ass.

My ass. I looked down at it now, thinking about it for the first time in days. It actually hurt from all the sitting. Maybe I'd go for a walk today. Yeah. I was tired of looking at this stretch of ocean. Maybe it looked different from the north. Sure it did. Why not? I got up, leaving my T-shirt on for some sun protection, and started to walk.

Huh. My legs actually worked. Even after five—no, six—days with no food, my muscles still worked. They were a little—whoa there—wobbly, but they worked. I walked along the beach, my feet crossing over each other as I stumbled along trying to keep balance, and looked around, feeling quite proud of myself.

I was still alive. Ha! Take that kidnappers. Still alive. Maybe it was my butt that was feeding me. I always thought it was kind of round. I bet my body was eating up all the fat stores from my butt now. Yeah. See, having a big ass is a good thing. Good, good, good. They should put that in magazines. Why diet? Why stay thin? If you ever get kidnapped and left for dead, your fat ass could save your life!

A light breeze blew my hair across my face and suddenly I felt dizzy. I put my hands out in front of me, but the beach tilted and spun. My sore butt hit the sand hard, radiating pain up my spine. I blinked a few times, trying to get my bearings. Then I laughed.

A breeze had blown me over. Things could not be good if a little breeze could knock me down like that. I rolled over onto my stomach, folded my arms in the sand, and rested my forehead on my forearms. Probably the backs of my legs were a lot whiter than the fronts. Maybe I should just lie here and even out the color.

Red in front, red in back.

I laughed even harder. Laughed until I coughed. Coughed until I was gasping for air. My throat constricted, my lungs burning with pain. Was this it? Was this dying? I tried to push myself up on my elbows, but my muscles quivered and I face-planted in the sand. Sucked sand into my mouth with the next cough. Gagging. Gagging. Gagging. I rolled onto my side. Heaved. Spit sand everywhere. Convulsing, drawing my knees up toward my chest. Tears streamed down my face into the sand.

Dying. This was me, dying.

"Reed."

I blinked. Covered my mouth with my hand to try to quiet the cough. Surely I was imagining things. I had not just heard my name.

"Reed."

I squeezed my eyes shut. I was hallucinating. Dammit. I really was dying. How many times could one person die?

"Reed. Up here. Look up."

It was Thomas. Son of a bitch. Thomas was here. So maybe I was already dead.

"Come on, New Girl," he said, his voice teasing. "You can do it."

I rolled over onto my stomach again and looked up in the direction from which I thought the voice was coming. Looked at the tree line, just a few feet away, and gasped. Blue eyes stared back at me from the darkness of the forest. Thomas's blue eyes.

Had God sent him here to take me to heaven? Because if I was going to go, that would be a really cool way to go. But wait, Thomas had not, technically, been the most pious do-gooder on earth, what with the drug dealing and the lying and the short-temper problem. Had he even *gone* to heaven? Crap. What if he was here to take me to hell?

"You're not dead, Reed. Just come here."

"I can't," I said.

My arms were so weak they felt like noodles. There was sand in my mouth, up my nose, in my eyelashes.

"Yes, you can. You can do anything," Thomas said. "I've been watching you, Reed. You have no idea how strong you are."

"But I—"

"Just come here," Thomas said, growing impatient. "There's something I want to show you."

Well. That was intriguing. My dead ex-boyfriend had something he wanted to show me? I mean, who could turn down an offer like that? I braced my hands under me and pushed as hard as I could, lifting myself up onto my knees. The head rush was excruciating and long. Way too long to be normal. But eventually, my vision cleared and I could make out shapes and colors again. Thomas was still there, his blue eyes peeking out at me now, from under a low bush.

I squinted. How could he be that low to the ground?

Edging forward on my knees, I called out to him. "Thomas? What are you doing? I so don't have the energy for hide-and-seek."

I shoved the low, thick leaves of the bush aside and gasped. The blue was not Thomas's eyes. It was the label on a bottle of Evian water. I grabbed it, fully expecting it to disappear right in front of me, but it didn't. I was holding an actual bottle of water. A full bottle of water.

But no. It wasn't possible. This island was deserted. I hadn't seen a soul, a boat, anything, in six days. This was just another hallucination. A really horrible one, since I could feel the plastic beneath my fingers.

"This isn't real," I told myself.

"Yes, it is."

Thomas was right beside me now. His voice in my ear.

"No. It's not." Tears coursed down my face. "And you're not either. I'm going insane."

"You're not. Just open it. Drink it," Thomas said. "But take sips. You don't want to throw up again."

My hands trembling, I opened the bottle. Heard the click as the cap released from its plastic band. I had never wanted anything so badly in my life, but I was afraid. Afraid that I would lift the bottle to my lips and the whole thing would vanish.

"Here. I'll help you," Thomas said.

He lifted the bottle to my lips. Tipped it toward my mouth.

Cool water ran over my cracked lips and down my throat. The relief was instantaneous. I wanted to gulp the whole thing down, but remembered what Thomas had said and stopped. I didn't want to retch it up. Not only that, but I had to conserve it. Make it last as long as possible. I lowered the bottle and took a breath. Then I allowed myself one more gulp. My tears turned to tears of joy. Relief.

Thank God for people who littered.

People who littered. People.

This meant someone had been here before. It meant people did, occasionally, come to this island. Someone knew it was here. And if someone knew it was here, it was possible they were coming back.

It was possible that even if the kidnappers had left me for dead and Upton had forsaken me and Noelle had given up on me, I could still be saved.

I looked at Thomas, wanting to share the good news, but he was gone.

Of course he was. He was never there.

I looked down at the bottle and cap clutched in my ragged, dirty hands. But if he was never there, how did I find this?

I felt a chill and looked around. "Thanks," I said, just in case. "I'm glad you're watching over me."

Then I capped the bottle, got up, and set off to find some food already. I was not going to end up like Thomas. I wasn't going to let some sadistic psycho remove me from this earth before I was ready. I was going to find a way off this island. And if I died in the process, at least it would be on my terms.

THIS CLOSE

I walked north on the beach, farther than I had walked on any of the previous days. If someone had dropped a water bottle, who knew what else they had dropped? Maybe they were even still here somewhere. Maybe I was about to stumble upon a group of college students camping out on the beach. And they would have food. And more water. And a boat.

A girl could dream.

As I strode along, ignoring the weakness in my limbs, the shakiness of my knees, I kept one eye on the beach up ahead and another on the tree line, looking for more lost goodies. A can of Pringles would be nice. Or maybe a McDonald's bag with an Egg McMuffin inside?

Up ahead, a long branch hung out over the beach in an arc. As I approached I realized why. It was heavy with fruit. *Laden* with little green apples. My heart leapt as I dropped my bottle of water in the sand and ran forward. Overjoyed and cursing myself at once, I pulled the branch toward me. If only I had come this far a few days ago. I could have been feasting on fruit all this time.

I yanked an apple down. My stomach grumbled in anticipation as I brought it to my lips. In that split second I imagined the sugary sweetness. The juice running down my throat. My mouth actually began to water. God, this was going to feel so . . . so . . . good. I opened my lips and was about to bite into the apple, when my eyes fell on the tree's trunk and I froze. My mind flashed on the manchineel tree in the Ryans' garden—the gray bark, the shiny green leaves, the yellowish-green fruit—and the apple dropped from my fingers. This was the same type of tree. I turned around and sprinted for the ocean. Dropping to my knees, I shoved my hands under the water and scrubbed them together. Mrs. Ryan had said that just touching the sap could be deadly.

I had just come *this close* to eating an actual poisoned apple.

Who was I? Snow White?

Shaking violently, I lifted my hands in front of my eyes and stared at my fingers. They looked okay. Burned and cracked, but okay. My flesh wasn't melting from my body or anything. The waves crashed around me, soaking the hem of my T-shirt and the dress underneath, but for a long moment I didn't move. I took a deep breath and allowed my pulse to calm.

I was okay. Still stranded, still starving, but okay.

Slowly, I stood up and turned around. A thought ever so languidly formed itself in the back of my addled mind. Maybe I couldn't eat the apples, but that didn't mean I couldn't use them.

I walked back up the beach and slipped the bandana off my head. Tying the two free corners together, I fashioned a little sack. Then I untied my blindfold from my wrist and used it to protect my hand as I picked as many apples as I could load into the sack. I grabbed my water bottle up from the sand as I walked by and headed back for my little stretch of beach.

If those guys did come back, I was going to be ready.

SAVE MYSELF

The sun was starting to go down. I sat atop the rock jetty, the one that was home to the barnacles I had used to fray the twine from my wrists that first day, and watched as hundreds of brilliant colors lit the horizon. I ran my fingers over the six lines in my piece of drift. I had so hoped there would never be a seventh, but if I made it through this night, it seemed as though there would be.

Pulling my knees up under my chin, I yanked the hem of the T-shirt down over my legs to my ankles, affording myself the slightest bit of warmth. Next to me on the rocks was my bottle of water, still almost full, my pile of manchineel apples, my purse, and my one shoe. I don't know why I felt the need to keep these things near me at all times, but I did. Having them near me made me feel more secure.

As the sun dipped toward the ocean, painting the sky with bright pinks, purples, peaches, and yellows, I took a deep breath and tried to fend off a niggling feeling of fear and desperation. Another day was ending. Another night about to begin. How long could I make it without food? I wanted to survive. Wanted so badly to get off this island and see my family and my friends again. But just wanting it wasn't going to make it happen.

Behind me, the palm trees danced in the wind, their fronds click-clacking against one another. It sounded like a thousand mini-stilettos crossing a marble floor. I closed my eyes and pretended I was at a fancy Billings function. That I could hear the sound of my friends' laughter and conversation. The sounds of champagne corks popping and glasses clinking and cell phones trilling. A smile twitched at my lips. What were London and Vienna doing right now? Were Kiki and Constance still hanging out in New York? I bet Astrid was going balls-out crazy in London, doing whatever she could to piss off her parents. I rested my cheek on my folded arms and sighed, wishing I was with them. Any of them. All of them. Wishing I was anywhere but here.

The wind died, and for a moment there was silence. But I kept my eyes closed, clinging to the happy, warm images of my friends. And that's when I heard it.

A motor. A boat engine. Far off, but getting closer. Undoubtedly getting closer. My heart slammed into my rib cage like a rock off a slingshot and my head popped up, eyes wide. It had been so long since I'd heard anything other than the sounds of nature, I thought my brain was playing tricks on me. I scanned the water anyway. It was already much darker than it had been just moments before, but I saw the shadow of something moving out there on the ocean. Saw the white foam of wake made by a vessel cutting through the water. My heart leapt and I was on my feet.

It was Upton. It had to be. He was coming to save me. I lifted my arms over my head and waved them around like a crazy person. Which, of course, I was. A few hours ago I'd been talking to a dead guy.

The boat drew closer. Soon I was able to make out its shape. It was a small speedboat, nothing fancy, and there were two people at the helm. Not one, but two. And neither of them was Upton. I would have recognized his shadow. The line of his shoulders. The lift of his chin.

No. It was the kidnappers. They were back. My hope fizzled like a fourth of July sparkler being shoved into sand. If they were back, they were here to kill me. I looked down at my pile of apples and my jaw clenched with grim determination. It was up to me. I was the only one who could save me now. Using my handy bandana sack, I gathered up the apples and jumped down to the sand to greet my executioners. I had promised myself I would be ready when they returned, and I was. But knowing that didn't stop nervous bile from rising up in my throat.

My plan had to work. It just had to.

They beached their boat and hopped out into the shallow water. Their faces were still obscured by wiry beards and dark sunglasses. As they slowly approached, I reached into my sack of apples with my bandaged hand and drew one out, clutching it behind my back.

"Well, well. Look who's a little survivor," Red Beard said.

They were both smiling. *Had* Upton doubled their money? Were they here to bring me back? My heart pounded with adrenaline, hope, and exhaustion. I gripped the apple as tightly as I could, holding on to it for dear life. As if it could save me. I hoped it could save me.

"Where's Upton?" I asked, trying to remain positive.

They laughed. Red Beard drew a sweaty hand across his face, wiping under his nose. Both of them, in fact, were beaded with perspiration. Their fake beards were probably itchy and suffocating. Why did they feel the need to disguise themselves? I barely knew anyone on St. Barths. And if they were going to kill me, I'd never have the chance to identify them anyway.

"What's so funny?" I asked, my heart pounding so hard now I shook with each beat.

"Your little boyfriend never paid," Mr. Stilted English said.

A gray cloud obscured my vision, and it took a long moment for me to realize it wasn't actually there. That I had just come this close to fainting dead away.

"He . . . but you went to him? You told him where I was, what you were going to do?" I rambled. Behind me, the apple jumped around in my hand. Upton couldn't leave me here for dead. He just couldn't.

But obviously, he had. What motive did these two have to lie? Hot tears welled up in my eyes. How could I have believed Upton when he told me he loved me? I had believed he wanted to be my boyfriend. I had almost slept with him. Sawyer was right about him. He didn't deserve a girl like me.

"He decided it was a better idea to go to the police," Mr. Stilted English told me, taking a step forward.

My desperate rambling thoughts were brought up short. Okay.

Well, maybe Upton wasn't all bad. Going to the police wasn't as bad as ignoring the situation completely, right? But if he really loved me, why bother? Why not just pay?

"How do you know he went to the police?" I asked. Not that I cared. I was just stalling for time. The longer we stood there, the more the real reason for their visit sank in. Somewhere, one of them was concealing a gun. The gun that held the bullet that was going to kill me.

There was another laugh. "Because we *are* the police." Stilted English finally lost the stilt and went back to his regular voice, his French accent.

"Surprise, Miss Brennan!" Red Beard added.

In a rush, I realized who they were. Red Beard was Officer Marshall, and Stilted English was Officer Gravois. The cops from the hospital. The ones who had found my assertions so amusing. The ones who assumed I was a spoiled brat who was not, in fact, being stalked by a murderer.

They were going to murder me. Oh, the irony.

The two of them approached me now, slowly, predatorily, like lions stalking a gazelle. I took an instinctive step back. Officer Marshall stopped in his tracks.

"Wait. She has something behind her back."

Gravois lifted his dark glasses and eyed me with suspicion. "What are you hiding, eh? Some kind of homemade weapon?"

I let out a shout as I flung the apple at Marshall with all my might. Thanks to my weakened state, it made a pathetic arc in the air and landed in his ready hand. He snorted a laugh.

"What did you think you were going to do? Knock me out with your superhuman strength?"

He tossed the apple up and down a few times. I watched him play his little game and held my breath. He was going to throw it over his shoulder, or down on the ground. What had I been thinking? This was never going to work. What were the chances that he would actually—

Then he lifted the apple to his lips and took a bite.

My heart leapt with joy. I couldn't have asked for a more perfect moment. Right now he was chewing on poison. The juice trickled down his chin. How long would it take before he keeled over dead? I had to be ready. Had to use the moment of surprise to take on kidnapper number two. Marshall chewed, swallowed, wiped the back of his hand across his mouth.

Come on manchineel. Work your magic.

But nothing happened. He just licked his lips and tossed the rest of the apple in the sand. Nothing.

My shoulders sagged along with all my hopes. Had Mrs. Ryan been lying when she told us about the dangers of the tree? Was she just that morbid that she wanted to scare us for no reason? Or had I been wrong about the tree? Was it just some ordinary crab apple?

"Say your good-byes, kid," Officer Marshall said.

He drew a gun out of the back waistband of his pants and pointed it at my chest. My breath stopped in my throat. These were the last few beats of my heart. The cold sand beneath my feet was the last thing I would ever feel.

I was about to close my eyes and see whatever it was my sub-conscious wanted me to see in my last moments, when suddenly Officer Marshall's eyes rolled into the back of his head and he crumpled to the ground. His whole body started to shake, and drool poured out the corner of his mouth. Both Gravois and I were so stunned that for a moment, neither one of us moved. But then my eyes flicked to the gun, which was now twitching like mad, Marshall's fingers curled around the handle. Gravois saw it, too, and at the same time, we lunged.

Except I had another surprise in store for him. Rather than lunging for the gun, I grabbed my piece of driftwood. Gravois was still struggling to release the gun from his buddy's convulsing grip when I ran over to him, wielding the driftwood like a baseball bat. I was mere inches away when he finally freed the gun. He looked up, and his eyes widened. He started to lift the weapon as I let out a guttural scream and swung. The driftwood slammed into his skull with a satisfying crack. His neck twisted at an unnatural angle and he slumped over the now still body of his partner. I stood over them, my chest heaving with each and every breath, as I started to comprehend what I had just done.

At least one of them was dead. Maybe both. I had just saved my own ass. Who needed Upton Freaking Giles?

I turned and ran for the boat, tripping through the water. All I had to do was shove the thing off the sand, climb in, and get the hell out of here. We couldn't be that far from St. Barths if they'd taken this tiny vessel from there. I could find it. I'd have to find it. I clutched the sleek white side of the boat and was about to start pushing it away from the shore, when I glanced inside and my heart stopped.

The keys were not in the ignition.

"*Ma petite!* Where do you think you are going?"

The voice sent a sickening shiver down my spine. I turned around and swallowed hard. Gravois pushed himself to his knees and rose shakily to his feet. He held his head with one hand and lifted the gun with the other.

Dammit, Reed. What was the one lesson learned from watching all those horror movies with Scott and his friends?

The villains are never as dead as you think they are.

HERE

Suddenly, there was a huge roar, like another boat bearing down on me from behind. Gravois's jaw dropped. All my hair blew in front of my face, whipping into my eyes. Disoriented, I felt my pulse start to race. Gravois still had a gun, and now I couldn't even see.

As the roaring grew louder, I was knocked off my feet by a stiff wind. A gunshot split the air and I gasped in a breath before dropping down under the water. The cool waves enveloped my hot skin as I scrambled backward into deeper water. Once I was there I stayed down. I had no idea what was going on, but I knew Gravois was shooting. If I stayed beneath the surface, maybe he wouldn't be able to get a good shot.

Shoving my hair out of my face under the water, I blinked my eyes open and looked around. I could make out the fuzzy outline of the underside of the boat, and I started to swim around it. If I could just put the vessel between myself and Gravois, I'd at least have something to take the bullets for me.

Another shot. The bullet whizzed by me underwater, sending up a cloud of sand. My heart caught. I swam with all my might, my lungs bursting from the strain, and grappled my way to the other side of the boat. When I got there, I burst through the surface. I had to. My needy lungs were begging for air. The sky was completely dark now and I was crouched in shallow water between my jetty and the boat. From the shore, I heard shouts, but the roaring was gone. What the hell was going on? Who was shouting? Had Marshall woken up? And what the hell *was* that roaring sound?

Another shot sounded and I sucked in a breath. Down I went. I huddled next to the boat underwater. Gravois was obviously wasn't going to quit until he finished the job. What was I going to do? I couldn't stay down here forever. Couldn't even stay for another ten seconds. I needed to breathe. I needed to live. I needed a miracle.

And then, strong arms closed around me from behind and yanked me toward the surface. I let out a scream of terror, thrashing my legs and arms, trying to get free. But it was no use. Gravois had me. His grip was so tight I couldn't even begin to move. It was over. I had tried. I had tried so hard to stay alive these last few days, but it was over. At least I would go down fighting.

"Reed. Reed! Stop! It's me! Calm down!"

Suddenly, all my limbs went limp. I hung there, like a rag doll, his strong arms around my chest.

"Upton?" I whimpered.

His breath was ragged in my ear, but I could smell him. The clean, island scent of him. I leaned back against him, tears coursing down my face.

"You're not really here," I sniffled. "I'm hallucinating again."

"Can you stand?" he asked.

I couldn't answer. He placed me down in the water and my rubbery knees managed to keep me up. He kept one hand on my back as he walked around to face me, tilting my chin up so I was looking into his too-blue eyes. He had reddish-brown stubble all over his chin and cheeks and looked exhausted. Gray circles under his eyes. A pallor about his once tan skin.

"You're not hallucinating," he said. "I'm here."

My entire body collapsed. Deflated. Every ounce of adrenaline, gone. Upton caught me in his arms as my frail, parched, dried-up body heaved with sobs.

"It's okay. It's going to be okay now," Upton said.

I felt his arm slip under my back and he scooped me from the water as if I weighed nothing. He lifted one of my arms so that it was slung around his neck and I curled against his chest. I could hear his heart. He was really here. He'd come for me. He'd finally come.

As Upton walked up the beach, I blinked my eyes open. Several men surrounded Gravois and Marshall, securing handcuffs to their wrists. Marshall appeared to be alive, though still unconscious. I hadn't managed to kill either of them. Which I guess was a good thing. Although at that moment I wanted them dead. Wanted them dead more than I'd ever wanted anything in my life.

"Where're we going?" I asked as Upton walked away from my jetty, sticking to dry land.

"Helicopter," he said.

My head lolled back and I saw the blades overhead, jet-black against the dark sky. So this was where the roar had come from. That was what had knocked me off my feet. Upton handed me to another man who was crouching inside the helicopter. He deposited me on a vinyl bench and took my wrist between his fingers, feeling my pulse.

"Have you eaten anything since you've been here?" he asked.

I shook my head no.

"Drank anything?" he asked.

"Some water. Evian," I added needlessly.

"First thing we have to do is get her hydrated," the man said.

Upton had climbed in behind me and was sitting at the end of the bench. I felt dizzy lying on my back and sat up, curling against him.

"You really should lie down, miss," the man said.

I let out a noise that was somewhere between a whimper and a growl.

"Can't you start an IV from here?" Upton asked, laying a protective arm down my side.

There was a pause. "Certainly, sir."

"What's going on?" I croaked as someone barked an order and someone else rummaged around behind me. All I could see from my point of view was the white cloth of Upton's shirt, his forearm, and his big, silver watch. I didn't care to see anything else. If I could stay in this position forever, that would be just fine.

"They're going to feed you through an IV," Upton said, running his hand gently over my hair.

"No, I mean . . . where have you been?" I asked, blinking back tears. "I've been here for five . . . six . . . days? Where have you been?"

Upton's grip on me tightened. I could feel his tension throughout his body. "I'm so sorry, Reed. You have no idea. . . . When those men approached me, I didn't know what to do. I didn't know if they were lying, or who was behind the whole thing. There was no telling whether they'd make good on our deal or simply take the money and leave you for dead. So I hired this team of investigators to find you, but we kept coming up against brick walls, dead ends. Finally we thought we would simply follow them back to you when they came, but it took them this long. . . . I'm so sorry. I've been doing everything I can to find you."

He shifted his position and I found myself gazing out the open side of the helicopter. Marshall and Gravois were being dragged off toward a waiting boat.

"Who hired them?" I asked, clutching Upton's shirt as the EMT lifted my other arm to try to find a good vein.

"They think it was Poppy," Upton said grimly. "They found a disposable cell phone in her bag and all the calls were to the same number . . . a pay phone near the police station. They're questioning her now, back on the island. I'm so sorry I didn't believe you. I never thought she could do something like this."

Poppy. I had thought it was Paige and Daniel, hadn't I? But now I couldn't for the life of me remember why. And I didn't care. If it was Poppy, it was Poppy. It made sense. She hated me, was obsessed with Upton, and had money to burn. I couldn't wait to see her rot in jail.

"All right, sir, we're ready to go," someone said.

"Good. Let's get out of here." Upton's voice rumbled in his chest beneath my cheek.

The door shut.

"You're going to have to sit up or lie down, miss," the EMT said.

I sat up. "I don't want to go to the hospital." It was there that I'd met Gravois and Marshall.

The EMT shot me an impatient look. "You need immediate care."

"No. I'm not going back there," I said, my heart fluttering with nerves. "I can't. I don't trust them. I don't trust the people there. Upton, I—"

"It's okay," he said, running his hand gently over my hair. "Noelle's father has arranged for private care at his home." He looked over my head at the EMT. "We should have an ambulance waiting for us at the Ryans' to take her back to the Langes'."

"The Ryans?" I squeaked.

"This is their helicopter, and they have the only helipad on the island," Upton explained.

I swallowed hard. The very idea of being in the Ryans' house made my blood run cold. I didn't trust those people either. But if there was an ambulance waiting there, I wouldn't have to be there long. Noelle's family was going to take care of me. Of course they were.

The EMT started my IV as Upton placed a set of huge headphones over my ears. My weakened neck could barely hold up their weight. I leaned my head against the window and looked out at the island. I hated this place. Hated it with a vengeance. But at the same time it had been my home for almost a week. It was the place where I had almost given in to despair and death, but had fought back.

The helicopter's engine roared to life, the blades starting out with a slow, whomping sound and gradually quickening to a deafening growl. The headphones dulled it, but they also made it impossible to hear anything else. Next to me, Upton settled in, his arm clamped around my shoulders like he would never let go again. We rose slowly into the air, the ground dropping away from us until I could see the entire island.

It was small. And the area of beach I had explored was about all the sand there was. The rocky steppe extended all the way around the rounded south edge of the island, and to the north, the forest eventually took over the beach, the trees reaching all the way out to the water.

As the helicopter lurched forward, flying low over the darkened water, I looked back at the island, at my beach. I could have sworn I saw Thomas standing there in his white T-shirt, smiling at me as he waved good-bye.

FACE-OFF

The stretcher was lifted out of the helicopter and wheeled down a slight hill toward the Ryans' estate. It was pitch dark out now and the walls of the sprawling mansion were eerily white against the raven sky. I was on my back, the IV being wheeled next to me, soft white blankets tucked in around me, but I was still shivering violently. It had started about halfway through the trip back to St. Barths and hadn't slowed since.

Still, I felt more awake than I had in days. More present. More alert. Whatever was in the IV, it was working.

"Is Noelle here?" I asked Upton, who walked beside the stretcher.

We were coming around the side of the house now, headed for the back patio near the pool. The stretcher's wheels hit the stone patio and the ride quickly became a lot less smooth.

"She's on her way," Upton said, looking down at me. "Everyone's at Mrs. Lange's charity thing, but they're all coming here to see you."

I smiled grimly. Leave it to the Billings Girls and their friends to keep the party going even when one of their own has been missing for six days. Not that I could blame them. I'd attended the Legacy while Thomas was missing, hadn't I? That was how these people dealt with tragedy. They partied it away. At least Upton hadn't decided to attend. I guess he really had been focused on finding me.

"There you are!"

Mrs. Ryan came skittering over the patio from the house, her high heels clicking on the stone floor. In seconds she was looming over me, her auburn hair falling forward over her cheeks. She was wearing a dark green strapless gown and a wide gold necklace. Her face was the picture of concern.

"My God, Reed. Are you all right?" she asked, her hand to her chest.

"Yes," I said. "I think so. Thanks for the ride."

Her brow creased in confusion, but then she laughed. "Oh, the helicopter. Of course." She looked at Upton as we all continued inside the house, the EMTs still pushing my stretcher. "Some woman from the police station just called and said the ambulance was delayed, but it would be here within the next half hour."

"It was supposed to be waiting," Upton said, his jaw clenched.

"Well, you know how things work on this island," Mrs. Ryan said, rolling her eyes. "She also said they need you down there. They have some questions about Poppy and your . . . relationship."

"Now?" Upton was annoyed.

"It seems they want to wrap this up as quickly as possible," Mrs. Ryan said.

"Upton, I don't want you to go," I said.

"Don't worry. Let's just get you inside," he replied.

Once we were inside the house, there were a lot of hushed conversations between Mrs. Ryan and Upton and the EMTs, all taking place while I lay flat on my gurney, shivering and staring up at an ornate chandelier made out of coral and rock. Finally, the EMTs left in a huff. All I heard them say was that they highly recommended I visit the hospital within the next twenty-four hours.

"Can we get this thing out of my arm now? It's burning," I said, shoving the covers off of me and swinging my bare legs around the side of the stretcher. I got a head rush and brought my free hand to my forehead, waiting for it to pass.

Okay. So maybe the hospital would have been a solid idea.

"Of course," Mrs. Ryan said, rushing forward.

She helped me remove the bandage and the needle and pushed the IV tower aside. Ever since I'd arrived on this island she'd been nothing but a bitch to me. Perhaps she was feeling guilty now that I'd almost died for the fourth time. Now that one of her friend's daughters had hired hit men to kill me.

"What do you need?" she asked, stepping back, lacing her fingers together.

I glanced over her shoulder at Upton. "Food? Water? What first?" he asked.

"Actually, I'd kill for something solid to eat," I said. "And a bath would be great."

"I have this amazing bubble bath with aloe in it," Mrs. Ryan said. "It will do wonders for that burn."

"Let's get her upstairs," Upton suggested. "Then you can come down and talk to the chef."

"What about the police?" Mrs. Ryan asked him. "They said it was urgent."

Upton glanced at me warily. "I don't think I should go anywhere just now."

"Nonsense," Mrs. Ryan said. "I'm perfectly capable of taking care of Reed until you get back. Besides, the ambulance will be here soon, not to mention the rest of your friends and their families." She gave me a tight smile. "Everyone wanted to be here to make sure you're all right."

I swallowed hard as I looked at Upton. I didn't want him to go. Not after longing to see him for the past six days. I never wanted to let him out of my sight again. But if Noelle and the others were on their way, I could manage. Especially if he was going off to slam the last nail into Poppy's coffin.

"Reed?" he said.

"It's okay," I said as my bare feet hit the cold tile floor. My knees collapsed underneath me and Mrs. Ryan held me up. She was a lot sturdier than she appeared.

"Are you all right?" Upton asked.

"Fine," I said, clearing my parched throat. "You can go. Just . . . come right back," I said, glancing warily at Mrs. Ryan.

Upton approached me. He placed his hands gently on my shoulders, probably afraid of hurting my scorched skin. "Are you sure?"

"I'm sure," I said, not feeling sure at all.

"All right, then. I'll be back before you know it. And don't worry. Calista will take good care of you."

Since when did he call her Calista? I glanced at Paige and Daniel's mother. Yesterday, this morning even, I had been certain her children were trying to off me. But it wasn't Paige and Daniel. It was Poppy. Upton and his crack team of investigators were convinced it was Poppy.

"Come on," Mrs. Ryan said, flicking her fingers at me. "You'll feel so much better once you get in that bath."

I took a deep breath. If Upton trusted her, I supposed I should, too. Besides, like he said, Noelle would be here soon. And Kiran, Taylor, Tiffany, and the rest. If I could survive six days on a deserted island, I could survive six minutes with Mrs. Ryan.

"Okay."

Upton kissed me on the forehead and I was on my way. Mrs. Ryan kept one arm around my back, supporting me as I slowly climbed the wide, red-tile stairs. The second floor was carpeted, and the warm fibers were like heaven for my cold feet. She led me down the hallway to the very end, where an open room awaited us.

"This is my dressing room," she said, flicking on the light.

The chamber was actually one huge closet lined with shelves and drawers and racks of clothing built into the walls. At one end was a huge vanity table with curled legs and marble detailing. The mirror

was so tremendous I could see my entire body reflected in its surface. It was not a pretty sight. My face was such a dark red it seemed
unnatural, and my lips were cracked and crusted with blood. My hair
was a tangled, matted mess and hung limply over my shoulders. The
skin on my legs and arms had peeled in several places, leaving streaks
of mottled white against the bright red. Flecks of dead skin were pep-
pered everywhere.

If Upton still loved me after seeing me like this, it would be a
miracle.

"Have a seat and I'll draw the bath," Mrs. Ryan said, depositing
me on the soft velvet bench in front of the mirror. She opened a set
of double doors to my right, revealing a huge white bathroom. From
my angle I could see only a wide sink, but she disappeared to the right
side of the door and I heard her rummaging around. Heard the water
start to gurgle.

A bath was going to feel so good. Just sitting there in that clean,
airy room, I was starting to smell myself, and it was not a nice scent. I
wondered if Upton had noticed it on our way back from my island. If
he had, he'd been too polite to so much as wrinkle his nose.

Unable to stare at my horrifying reflection any longer, I turned my
attention to the myriad products on the table. There were bottles and
tubs and tubes and glosses. Moisturizers and toners and bronzers and
plumpers. I ran my trembling fingers along the beveled edge of the
table, unable to believe I was here. Back in civilization.

"Reed, I'm going to go check on the food," Mrs. Ryan called out.
"I'll be right back."

A door closed. An outside door to the hallway from the bathroom no doubt. I glanced over my shoulder at the open door, then reached for a bottle of perfume near the center of the table. I removed the glass top, intending to give myself a little spritz to mask my stench, when the scent of the perfume filled my senses and the room began to spin.

It was the scent I had smelled just before I was shoved off the stern of the Ryans' boat. Unmistakable. It brought me right back to that terrifying moment as if it were happening all over again.

The bottle fell from my quaking fingers and hit the table top with a crash. I was on my shaky feet like a flash, the adrenaline that had kept me alive on the island returning full force. Desperately, my eyes scanned the shelves and racks on the walls all around me, taking in flowered dresses and pressed pants and silky blouses. I took a deep breath and told myself to concentrate. If it was here somewhere, I could find it. I just had to concentrate.

I breathed in and slowly scanned the room. Right next to the two floor-to-ceiling racks of shoes was a small section of workout gear. Yoga pants were folded neatly on shelves. Tank tops hung on silver hangers. Right next to a half dozen hooded sweatshirts. My legs quaking, I stepped ever so slowly toward the rack. I saw the white trim before I was even halfway there, but I kept moving. I needed to be sure. My arm was so weak as I reached for the garment, I could barely lift the hanger off the high rod. But I managed. I drew the sweatshirt toward me and lifted the hood. The white trim traveled up the sleeve, along the shoulder, and all the way around the hood. It was the sweatshirt my attacker had worn.

But Mrs. Ryan? Why?

I heard a creak and whirled around. Mrs. Ryan was standing, framed by the doorway, with a heaping tray of food in her hands. Bread and cheese and grapes and apples.

Little green manchineel apples.

"Reed?" she said, glancing at the sweatshirt in my hands. "What are you—oh, are you cold?"

Why? Why was she trying to kill me?

She placed the tray on a small table near the door and as she did, her huge necklace shifted. My vision zoned in on it like heat-seeking radar. A gold necklace. A big, ornate gold necklace with thousands of tiny, sharp, gold leaves.

A bubble of disgusted realization welled up in my throat. Upton's first. Mrs. Ryan was Upton's first. No wonder he had called her Calista. They had been . . . intimate.

I was going to vomit. I had nothing in my system to vomit, but I was going to vomit just the same.

"Are you all right?" Mrs. Ryan asked. "The bath should be ready. Or do you want to eat first?"

She stopped short of lifting a poison apple toward me, but she might as well have. I took a step back, still clutching her sweatshirt in my hands.

"It was you," I said, my voice barely a whisper. "You hired those men to kill me."

A brief shadow of fear crossed over her face, which she quickly replaced with a look of total confusion. But it was too late. I had seen it. I had seen the recognition and I knew she was the one. And I also realized I should have kept my mouth shut—probably would have if I hadn't been so exhausted from my six days alone on a deserted island. Should have asked for a phone so I could call my parents and instead called the police. Because now I was alone with the person who had been desperately trying to kill me for days. Alone and weak.

But there was nothing I could do about that now.

"It's been you all along!" I said, still backing away. There was nowhere for me to go, except maybe the bathroom, but she could cut me off there by going back out into the hall and entering from the other door. I was trapped. Trapped with the woman who'd been trying to kill me for two weeks. The woman Upton had promised would take care of me.

Upton Giles was turning out to be a seriously bad judge of character.

"Reed, I don't know what you're talking about," Mrs. Ryan said, reaching up to toy with her necklace.

"You did it for him. Because you were jealous of Upton and me," I spat. "That is just sick, do you know that? He's friends with your *kids*. You're married!"

A flash of anger lit her eyes and she snapped. "Do not talk about what you could never understand!"

"You did it, didn't you?" I said, stalling for time now. Noelle and the rest of my friends would be here any second. Any second now. All I had to do was stay alive until they arrived. "You spooked my horse that day in the woods. And you rigged that Jet Ski to go haywire on me. And when neither of those little ploys worked, you shoved me off your boat and took my necklace so you could set up Marquis to take the fall. God, you must have been so frustrated when they found me alive," I said. "That must have just *killed* you."

Mrs. Ryan's face had taken on almost masklike calm, but her eyes quaked in their sockets. "You're going to have to stop saying things like that," she said, advancing on me. "We have a large staff in this house. Someone might hear you. Someone might actually repeat your delusional ramblings."

I glanced around at the dressing table for something I could use as a weapon. All I needed was something heavy. If I could take down Gravois, I could take down Mrs. Ryan. But there was nothing. Nothing but tiny gleaming bottles and tubes. Then something moved. Out in the hallway, I saw a shadow.

Please let it be Noelle or Upton and not Daniel or Paige or one of the other St. Barths nutbags.

"I'm not delusional," I said, the backs of my legs pressing into the dressing table. "And you're going to jail."

"Oh, really?" she said with a smirk. "What makes you think anyone's going to believe you? What makes you think I'm going to let you have a chance to make them?"

My heart stopped, but I managed to see the flaw in her plan. "If you hurt me, they're going to know it was you. Upton just left us alone together. You'll be the one and only suspect this time."

"Not if I left you alone in the tub for *just a few minutes* and when I came back you had drowned," she said through her teeth, her eyes wide with innocent wonder. "Who knows what kind of ailments six days of exposure on an island can cause? Heart attack, stroke, simple fainting . . . any one of these things could cause you to go under. So tragic, drowning in a marble tub after surviving all those days on the island."

Before I could even process the insanity of all this, she lunged at me and grabbed my hair in her hand. I shouted out in pain as she dragged me forward, toward the bathroom and the full tub. I struggled against her, but she was freakishly strong and I was pathetically weak. I screamed at the top of my lungs and before the sound even died away, Sawyer came bounding through the door with some kind of long object in his hand. He slammed the butt of it down on the back of Mrs. Ryan's skull. Her eyes popped open so wide I thought I might have to catch them in my palms, but then they closed and she crumpled forward onto the floor.

Sawyer and I stood there for a moment, both of us heaving for breath. Then he dropped his weapon at his feet—I could see now that it was some kind of modern table sculpture—and reached out a hand to me. He was wearing a black tuxedo, his long black tie loosened and askew.

"Are you okay?" he asked.

I tripped over Mrs. Ryan's ankle as I flung myself at him. Sawyer backed up a couple of steps from the force of my embrace, but I clung to him like there was no tomorrow.

"I can't take this anymore," I rambled. "I can't. I can't take it."

"It's okay. It's okay," Sawyer said, grasping the back of my T-shirt to hold me up.

"She did it. She tried to kill me," I said, glancing over my shoulder at Mrs. Ryan. "She set the whole thing up."

"I know. I heard everything," Sawyer said, pulling back so he could look me in the eye. "It's going to be all right." He shrugged out of his tuxedo jacket and slung it over my shoulders. The warmth was like nirvana.

I sniffled and nodded, still weak as could be. "What're you doing here?"

"Everyone's here," he said. "I was just the first one inside. Come on. Let's go downstairs and we'll call the police."

My eyes widened in terror.

"No. Not the police," he said quickly. "We'll call my dad. He'll know what to do."

"Okay," I said, clinging to him as we walked out to the hall. "And can we get something to eat? Something that's not poison?" I said, glancing at the tray on the table by the door.

Sawyer appeared confused, but nodded. "Absolutely. I think something that's not poison would definitely be a good idea."

FOOD

There was a lot of commotion. I could hear it from inside the airy kitchen with its bright aqua accents and gleaming silver appliances. I was eating a hunk of crusty bread with Sawyer and Noelle at my sides. Everyone else was out in the great hall at the front of the house, watching as Mrs. Ryan was hauled away in handcuffs. Mr. Lange had called the police after all. There was some shouting. A few slamming car doors. But I heard it all from inside a vacuum. It was over. It was finally over.

And I was finally eating.

"I don't believe this. This is actually beyond the scope of the believable," Noelle said.

She had brought me a black Calvin Klein sweat suit and didn't even care that I hadn't taken a bath before I put it on. Thanks to that and a pair of comfy white socks, plus the food and water, I had finally stopped shivering.

"Believe it, baby," I said, then snorted a laugh, my head jerking back slightly.

Noelle leaned toward me. Her black satin gown swished whenever she moved, and her heavy evening eye makeup seemed ridiculous to me in my haggard state. "You're delirious, aren't you? Doesn't she seem delirious?" she asked Sawyer.

"She was alone on an island for six days with nothing to eat and no one to talk to," Sawyer pointed out matter-of-factly.

"Point taken," Noelle said.

I wasn't delirious. I was just done. I couldn't wrap my brain around *another* near-death experience. Couldn't really feel it. Once I had stopped crying all over Sawyer and he'd found me something to eat, all the emotions had just sort of . . . stopped. Now all I could feel was the weakness, the exhaustion, the hunger, and the pain. Maybe once I solved all those issues, the emotions would crash in on me again, but for now, there was nothing.

"Is there more of this bread?" I asked, lifting the crusty bit I had left.

Noelle got up to cut me some more and brought back a cluster of grapes and a few slices of cheese with it. Someone had decided that bland was the way to go, but I would have pretty much killed for a chili cheeseburger. Or a pepperoni pizza. Or a huge pile of jelly donuts.

"So all this time it was Mrs. Ryan?" Noelle said as she placed the food in front of me on the glass-topped table and sat down again. "Why? Was she doing it for Paige?"

Sawyer and I looked at one another. If Noelle thought Mrs. Ryan's guilt was unbelievable, she was never going to be able to swallow her motive. I opened my mouth to respond, but a loud shout stopped me short.

"What the hell is going on here? Where's my father? You can't just drag her away like this! No! Get the hell off of me!"

It was Daniel Ryan. In one of his rages, it seemed. I heard scuffling footsteps. A crash. The clack of high heels. Suddenly Daniel and Paige came barreling into the kitchen, followed by Dash and Kiran. Daniel's otherwise handsome face was red with rage, his tuxedo tie still knotted tightly around his neck. Paige's auburn hair had come loose from its updo. The tail of her light green gown swished behind her as they stormed into the room.

"What kind of lies are you telling now?" Daniel shouted, getting right up in my face.

I instinctively skittered backward on my chair and ended up half in Noelle's lap, half suspended over the floor. He looked a lot like his mother did when she was getting all psychotic.

"First Poppy and now my mother? Who the hell do you think you are?"

"Your *mother* tried to kill Reed!" Sawyer shouted, getting up and shoving Daniel away from me with both hands.

Everyone fell silent. It was the first time I had ever heard Sawyer raise his voice. The first time he'd gotten directly involved in a conversation of his own volition, let alone a fight. We were all stunned. But it was Paige who recovered first.

"You're lying," she said, her voice quaking. "Why would my mother want to kill anyone, let alone *her*?" She gave me a look like I wasn't even worthy of her attention, let alone anyone's ire.

Just then a female police officer stepped into the room, a blue windbreaker over the standard uniform of polo shirt and shorts. Her short black hair was pulled back in a tiny, tight ponytail and she was looking at a small pad as she entered. After a moment she flipped the pad shut and glanced around at us.

"Paige and Daniel Ryan?" she asked.

"Yes," Daniel said, stepping forward with his sister.

"You're going to want to come down to the station to meet up with your father," the woman said. "Your mother has just confessed to attempted murder."

"What?" Daniel shrieked.

Paige clutched her purse in front of her with both hands. "I don't understand. She has no motive. She wouldn't hurt a fly. She—"

The woman sighed and flipped open her pad again to read. "Apparently she had some sort of sexual relationship with this girl's boyfriend . . . one Upton Giles?"

"Omigod." Paige turned around, and without so much as a breath, puked into the stainless steel sink. My stomach heaved. It was barely ready for food, let alone seeing someone else's come back up. I turned away and stared out the window toward the ocean.

"What?" Daniel blurted again. "No. That's not possible."

"That's what your mother says." The woman was behind me, but I saw her shrug, thanks to her reflection in the window. She looked at Paige and wrinkled her nose in disgust. "She didn't even need to be asked twice. It was almost like she was proud of it."

Kiran snorted a laugh and earned an admonishing look from the rest of us. "Sorry, it's just . . . I've done a few things in my life, but I've never shared a guy with my mom," she said, glancing at Paige's still heaving back.

Paige stood up straight, hand over her mouth, and ran out of the room in tears.

"She confessed?" Daniel said, staring at the officer. "To all of it?"

"Hiring the kidnappers, spooking the horse, rigging the Jet Ski," the woman said. "She does, however, maintain that this Marquis person is guilty of the incident at sea, but it seems like an open-and-shut case to me."

No one said a word. We all stared at the floor. Was Marquis really guilty, or had Mrs. Ryan hung him out to dry for some reason? I had no idea, and not enough energy to think about it for very long.

"This can't be happening," Daniel said.

As much as I disliked Daniel, I actually felt bad for him at that moment. It couldn't be easy to find out your mother was an attempted murderer. Not to mention a pedophile who'd had sex with one of your friends and was now obsessed with him.

"Are you coming along?" the woman asked him.

"I'll go get my sister," he said. Without another word, he ducked his head and walked out.

"Is there anything we can do for you, miss?" the woman asked me.

My brain was still fuzzy. I wanted to tell her she could put Marshall and Gravois in front of a firing squad, but somehow that didn't seem like the right thing to say.

"Where's Upton?" I asked.

"Sorry. I don't know," the officer replied.

"We'll take care of her," Noelle said. She moved as if to touch my back, but then thought better of it and placed her hand on the back of my chair instead. "She'll be fine."

The officer left and for a long moment there was no sound inside the kitchen aside from that of my own chewing.

"Upton's probably still downtown," Noelle said. "I'm sure he'll be back soon."

"So someone really was trying to kill you all this time," Kiran said finally. She tucked the skirt of her slim red gown beneath her as she lowered herself onto a chair in one elegant motion.

"Yep," I said.

"Reed, I'm so sorry we didn't believe you," Noelle said.

"Whatever," I replied. "Is there any more cheese?"

Dash rushed to get me some.

"Thanks," I said, shoving an entire slice into my mouth.

I could feel them all looking at one another with concern, eyeing me warily.

"Do you think she has post-traumatic stress disorder or something?" Kiran asked.

"You guys, I'm fine. I'm just starving. And I really want to take a bath and then slather myself in aloe," I said. "And then I want to sleep. For about two days."

"I think we can make that happen," Sawyer said.

"Dash, get your car," Noelle demanded, standing up with her hand on my back. "Let's get Reed home."

ADORABLE

I never saw the inside of the hospital. Mr. Lange hired a private nurse named Caroline and flew her in from the States. A big, comfy-looking woman, she was already at the house when we got back from the Ryans'. She got me cleaned up, aloed, and into bed in record time. Then she put in the call to my parents and handed me the phone so that we could all weep in relief together and make plans to see each other the second I was healthy enough to make the trip back to the States. All night long Caroline took my vitals and made me sip water here and there before I drifted back to sleep. She also had this carrot-scented balm that she applied to my entire body every hour on the hour. It felt amazing and it was actually healing my sunburn. I was still red, but it didn't hurt as much and it looked a lot less awful. Which was nice, since people kept dropping by to visit and I didn't like the idea of everyone seeing me looking like that horrifying dead girl from *The Ring*.

Caroline was also big on sleep. No one could stay for more than a few minutes, which was nice, because I definitely needed my z's. I was in such a deep sleep when Upton arrived the afternoon after Mrs. Ryan's arrest, I didn't even hear him come in, didn't know he was there, until Caroline woke me up trying to get rid of him. When I peeled my tired eyes open, she had one sturdy hand on his chest and was shoving him backward toward the door of my room.

"It's okay," I said, pushing myself up on my pillows. "Please. Let him in."

Caroline looked at me and *tsk*ed under her breath. "Mr. Lange said to give you whatever you wanted . . . but I'm coming back in fifteen minutes." She looked at Upton in a scolding way and lifted one chubby finger. "She needs her rest."

"Of course," Upton replied.

He had a glass vase full of lilies, which he placed on the table at my bedside. Then he took a step back as if afraid to get too close, shoving his hands into the back pockets of his jeans. He had shaved since I'd seen him last, but he still looked tired. Almost as tired as I felt.

"Are you sure this is all right?" he asked, his brow knitting.

"What?" I asked.

"Me being here," he said, his voice grave. "I'm sure you hate me, and with good reason. That's why I've stayed away. I assumed you didn't want to see me."

I blinked. "Why would I hate you?"

"Because this is all my fault," Upton replied, clearly distressed. "All of it. She was after you because of me."

I chuckled and pushed my hair back from my face with both hands. "Upton, it's not your fault she's crazy."

"But it is! You said it yourself the day after you got out of the hospital," he said, throwing out a hand and pacing away. "You said you weren't going to wait around for one of my jilted girlfriends to kill you and you were right. It just happened to be a girlfriend you didn't know about."

"Upton," I said calmly.

"I'm going to make this up to you, Reed. I swear it," he said. "If there's anything I can do—"

"Upton!"

"What?" He finally stopped moving, stopped rambling.

"Caroline's going to be back in thirteen minutes," I said. "Are you going to kiss me or what?"

Upton's entire face relaxed. He sat down on the bed next to me, touched my scorched cheek delicately with his palm, and kissed my cracked, blistered lips. It would have been romantic if it hadn't been so agonizing. I winced and pulled away.

"Okay, ow," I said.

"Sorry," he replied, biting his lip.

"Maybe just cuddling would be a better idea," I said.

"Sounds good to me." He leaned back against the headboard and pulled me toward his side, wrapping his arms around me. I nestled against him until my head was perfectly cradled in the crook of his arm, and took a deep, calming breath.

"So tell me, what's going on out there in the world?" I asked.

"Well, they let Poppy go," he said. "Apparently Calis—Mrs. Ryan—planted that cell phone in her bag."

"What about Red Beard and Stilted English?" I asked, fiddling with a fold in my sheet.

"Who?" he said.

"Marshall and Gravois," I clarified.

"Both alive. Though Marshall barely," he replied. "And both going to jail for a very long time."

"Good," I replied.

Upton lightly kissed the top of my head and sighed. "I just don't get it. That night, after she found us in her stateroom, we had this long conversation and I thought she was okay," Upton said. "She actually wished us every happiness and I believed her. And then, apparently, she turned around and shoved you off the back of the boat."

I shuddered and Upton held me a bit tighter. "Sorry," he said.

"It's okay," I replied. "I guess people do crazy things for love."

Upton laughed. "She never loved me. She was just obsessed."

"Oh, Upton. You're so adorable," I said, tilting my head up to look at him.

"Am I?" he said, raising his eyebrows.

"Haven't you figured it out yet?" I said. "Everyone loves you."

Upton pulled back a bit to see me better. "Even you?"

I sighed, my heart full. "Yes. Even me."

He smiled. "Oh, bollocks."

"What?" I asked.

"I'd really like to kiss you," he said.

I grinned and lifted my right arm. There was a wide band of white skin that had been protected by my blindfold most of my days on the island. "You can kiss me there."

He tilted his head, brought my wrist to his lips, and kissed the spot on the inside, right near the heel of my hand. A shiver of delight raced up my arm.

"Good?" he asked.

"Perfect," I replied.

So he kissed it again. And again and again and again. Until I dissolved in a fit of giggles and forgot all about the island, the kidnappers, the sunburn, and everything bad in the world.

ROOMIES

I rinsed the two-hundred-dollar-an-ounce moisturizing masque from my face and blotted my sensitive skin with a towel. When I looked into the mirror, Kiran was staring at me from over my shoulder, a red silk robe cinched around her waist. It was her product, after all, so she had a vested interest in making sure it had done the trick. Unfortunately, her disappointment was written all over her face.

"Well, at least we got your hair looking normal," she said in a resigned way.

"Shut up!" I said, whipping the towel at her.

"I'm just kidding!" she replied, her arms crossed in front of her face to protect herself. "You look a thousand percent better."

"Really?" I glanced at my reflection. After two days my face was almost entirely healed, except for my nose, which was red and peeling. My lips were still cracked and they stung 24/7, but the blisters were gone, which made eating a lot easier. And kissing. Which

Upton and I had tested out earlier that evening while Caroline was on a break.

"Really," Noelle said, appearing in the bathroom doorway. "By the time we get back to Easton you'll be almost recognizable."

Easton. A little shiver went through me at the thought of seeing Josh again. Had he heard about what had happened? I had a feeling that none of the girls had called him, and guys, as a rule, were less reliable gossips. I had to believe that if Dash, Gage, or West had reached him with the news he would have called me. Or at least e-mailed. But there was nothing. Over two weeks since I'd seen him and not one word.

Not that it mattered. I had Upton. And Upton was there for me every day.

"Come on. Taylor's mixed a special color for you and she won't shut up about it," Noelle said. She gathered her hair up atop her head and shoved a hair pick into it to hold it there. Which it miraculously did.

I followed her and Kiran back into my room, where Taylor, Tiffany, and Amberly were hanging out, flipping through magazines as Noelle's iPod blasted music from the dock on my dresser. Noelle had pulled in a few of the chairs from the dining room, and Taylor had set up a foot spa in front of one of them. Laid out on the floor was her professional manicure/pedicure kit with dozens of tools perfectly lined up and ready to go.

"I never understood why you learned to give pedicures," I said as I took a seat in the chair. The muscles in my feet let out an almost audible sigh as the warm, bubbly water closed around them. "Don't you guys all go to salons to get them done?"

"My mother has this woman Charlotte come in and do her nails every week, and when I was a kid I was kinda fascinated by it, so she taught me," Taylor said with a shrug. Her blond curls were held back with a skinny black headband, and she wore a black spaghetti-strap nightgown with eyelet cutouts at the hem. She grabbed the bottle of polish she had mixed for me and shook it up, inspecting it closely as the polishes incorporated.

"It came in handy at Billings when there was too much snow to go out and nothing else to do," Kiran said, dropping onto my bed and reaching for a chocolate from one of the many open boxes we had tossed there.

"Ah, Billings. I can't wait to get home," Tiffany said, tilting her head back as Amberly filed her fingernails.

Kiran and Taylor exchanged a look. They had left Billings last year, never to return. I wondered if, all protestations aside, they actually missed it. I'd only been kicked out for a month, and I definitely had.

"I've been thinking about it, and Reed, I think you should move in with me," Noelle said. She dropped onto the bed near the pillows, sending the boxes of chocolates—and Kiran—bouncing.

"What?" we all blurted in unison.

"You're going to give up your single?" Tiffany demanded, sitting up so fast Amberly dropped the emery board.

Noelle rolled her eyes like it was no big deal. "I can't make her and Amberly live together. They'll kill each other."

There was an uncomfortable silence, filled only by the sound of the bubbling foot spa. My last roommate had, after all, tried to kill me. At this point there could be a club—a small, very exclusive club—of people who'd tried to off Reed Brennan. I wondered what the meetings would be like—Ariana, Sabine, and Mrs. Ryan all gathered in the same room comparing notes. The very idea made me shudder.

"Bad choice of words," Noelle said. "But you know what I mean. We'll just move Astrid in with Amberly and get those girls out of that horrid triple, and Reed can live with me."

"Are you sure?" I asked.

"Clearly someone has to be looking out for you at all times," Noelle said, flipping open a copy of *Vanity Fair* on the comforter in front of her. "Who else is going to do it? Besides, if it wasn't for me convincing you to stay after the whole near-drowning episode, you wouldn't have even been here to get kidnapped. I think that makes you my responsibility."

She said this all very cavalierly, like it wasn't the biggest deal, but I knew her. I knew she never would have said a word about it if she didn't feel horribly guilty. Of course, it wasn't her fault. Not really. I made my own decisions. I was the one who had decided to stay. But I didn't say it. Dwelling on it would probably just piss her off.

Everyone looked at me. It was as if Noelle was asking me to the prom in front of all our friends and everyone watching was on the edge of their seats, wondering if I was going to break her heart. While I doubted that Noelle had anything emotionally invested in what I was going to say next, I felt suddenly nervous.

"Um, okay," I said.

"Cool!" Amberly blurted, then turned beet red.

Everyone laughed. Clearly she wanted to room with me about as much as I wanted to room with her. Suddenly I found myself looking forward to getting back to school. I couldn't wait to move back to Billings, to settle in with Noelle. Living with her was going to be amazing. I just knew it. And even if it wasn't, it couldn't be worse than living in that crappy single in Pemberly.

"Then it's settled. But I get the bed by the window," Noelle said, lifting a finger.

"Of course you do," Kiran replied with a touch of sarcasm.

"Oh, turn this up! I love this song!" Amberly gushed, waving a hand at the iPod.

Kiran got up and strolled over to the dock, cranking up the volume. It was some doofy pop song I couldn't believe Noelle had downloaded, but before I could make a crack about it, Amberly was singing along, bopping her head to the music as she filed Tiffany's nails. Soon the rest of us were watching her, trying not to burst out laughing so she would continue obliviously, amusing us for as long as possible. Finally she must have realized how quiet we had all become, because she looked up at us and turned pink all over again.

"What? I'm a *good* singer!"

We all burst out laughing, and Kiran tossed me a piece of chocolate. As I sat back to enjoy my pedicure, I looked around at my friends and realized this was the last time we'd all be together for a long time—maybe even forever. For a split second it felt like old times. Like the days when Ariana was my friend—before I knew what she had done to Thomas, before she had threatened my life. It felt like those rare nights when we were all hanging out, letting go, keeping the outside world at bay.

I missed those times. But maybe I could have them again. Not with the same people, of course, but still. I was headed back to school. Back to Billings. And while a lot of my relationships there needed some serious repairing, after everything I'd been through on this trip, the fact that my Billings sisters had wrongfully ousted me no longer seemed like the biggest deal.

Soon I would be home. I'd be back with my friends. With no one stalking me or trying to kill me or playing stupid pranks on me. My life had been saved on that island, and this was why. So that I could go back. So that I could go back to where I belonged.

NEW STUDENTS

Once again, my bags were piled by the door, but this time they were joined by Noelle's, tripling the size of the pile. We were going home this afternoon. Finally. When I had first arrived on St. Barths I couldn't imagine ever wanting to leave. Now every inch of my body itched for the door, the car, the plane. I just wanted to get back to normal.

Then Upton squeezed my hand. I looked at him and my heart contracted. "Can I take you with me?" I whispered.

"I wish I could come," he replied. "But I promise I'll visit you soon."

"No whispering at the table," Noelle interjected. "You two love-birds are so rude."

I blushed and glanced around at the parents on the other side of the brunch table, all of whom were now looking at us either with amusement or approbation. Noelle was obviously kidding, but it was still embarrassing.

"Reed, could you pass the fruit, please?" Sawyer asked, breaking the silence and giving me something to do. I released Upton's hand and passed Sawyer the big frosted-glass bowl.

"Thanks," he said, looking me in the eye.

I smiled back gratefully. "Thank *you*."

Mr. Lange cleared his throat and stood up from his seat at the end of the table. He was wearing a pink oxford shirt tucked into perfectly pressed chinos, looking every bit the casual businessman. As he stood, he lifted his mimosa glass at his side.

"Everyone, if I could have your attention for a brief moment, I have an announcement to make," he said.

I glanced past Upton at Noelle, who lifted one shoulder in bemusement. What was all this about?

"These last two weeks—the last few months, really—have been a trying time for all of us," Mr. Lange began, glancing in my direction. "But with a new year comes a fresh start, and the board of directors at Easton Academy has made a move that I believe will help usher in a whole new era at our beloved school."

Across the table from Graham and Sawyer, Mr. Hathaway was touching his napkin to his lips, clearly trying to hide behind it.

"I'm happy that you will all be the first to know that Spencer Hathaway has accepted the position of headmaster of Easton Academy," Mr. Lange announced. "And that his two fine boys will be the newest additions to the student body."

"No way," I blurted, looking at Sawyer. "You're going to Easton?"

Sawyer nodded, pushing his hands into the napkin across his lap.

The Langes and the Gileses applauded, and Upton got up to congratulate Mr. Hathaway. Noelle went over and gave Mr. Hathaway a kiss on the cheek, then paused by Graham's chair on the way back.

"You two sure you can hang with us?" she joked.

"I think we can handle it," Graham said, taking a bite of his bacon.

Sawyer didn't look quite as confident, though.

"What's wrong? Nervous about starting a new school?" I asked.

"I guess," he said, looking down at his plate. "It sucks, switching over midyear."

"Well, don't worry about it. You already have friends there, so that's a good thing," I said, glancing at Noelle. "And I'm sure with your dad as the headmaster, you guys will get placed in one of the good dorms."

"Which ones are the good ones?" Graham asked, on the edge of his seat.

Noelle lowered herself into Upton's now vacant chair to be closer to us. "Well, for guys it's Ketlar. You definitely want to be in Ketlar. If anyone utters the word *Drake*, run in the opposite direction."

"What's wrong with Drake?" Sawyer asked.

"Nothing," I said, rolling my eyes. "Everyone just *thinks* there is."

"Whatever," Noelle said. "Little Miss Brightside here likes to believe everyone is created equal. You'd think she'd be over that by now."

"What dorm are you guys in?" Graham asked, turning sideways in his chair, his sport jacket falling open to reveal his somewhat wrinkled white shirt.

"Billings House," I replied.

"*The* best house on campus. We'll introduce you to our house-mates. We have a few single girls on the prowl," Noelle added with a wink, taking a sip of her mimosa.

"Noelle? Could I see you for a moment, please?" Mrs. Lange asked from the other side of the table. Her cell phone was open and she held her hand over the receiver. "I'm on with Bliss and they need to update your information."

"Coming, Mother," Noelle replied.

I watched her go, wondering for the millionth time at the oddities of Mrs. Lange's behavior. Here she was, hosting a brunch—a celebratory brunch, as it turned out—and everyone was busy chatting up the guest of honor while she was on the phone booking spa appointments.

"You know, Noelle's dad and my dad were talking about Billings last night," Sawyer said, pushing his eggs around with his fork. "They were in my dad's office on the phone with someone on speaker. I could only hear one end of the conversation because the volume wasn't cranked up that loud, but the word *Billings* definitely came up a few times."

"What were they saying?" I asked.

"I don't know, but it didn't sound good," Sawyer replied, glancing warily at his dad and Mr. Lange. "Noelle's dad seemed pissed and my father kept trying to calm him down."

Suddenly my heart felt like it was shrinking inside of me, bouncing around like a Ping-Pong ball. What could this possibly mean? I leaned closer to the table and Sawyer, and kept my voice down.

"Can you remember anything specific? Were they talking about splitting us up?" I asked, my hand flat on the table, my palm sweating. Sawyer's eyes darted around, like he was suddenly nervous. My tension was rubbing off.

"I don't know. My dad kept saying, 'We understand,' over and over again. And there was something about a media crisis. . . ." He shrugged, but then his face lit up. "And oh yeah," he whispered. "Toward the end I definitely heard Noelle's dad agree it was for the good of the school. Although he didn't seem that happy about whatever it was."

I swallowed hard. Usually "for the good of the school" was not a good sign for the Billings Girls. I looked up at Noelle, who was chatting merrily with her mother, and a chill went through me. What had her dad and Mr. Hathaway decided with whoever was on the phone? And did she know about it?

I decided right then and there that I was not going to ask. If she didn't know about it, she would grill me for information I didn't have. It would be better to just wait until we were back at Easton. I was sure that whatever it was, we would find a way to fix it. We'd have to. There was no way I was going back to Pemberly. Not now.

Besides, maybe Sawyer had misheard. Or I was misinterpreting. Anything was possible. And it wasn't worth getting all stressed over without knowing the details.

"Hey."

Upton's warm hand touched the back of my neck and his other hand clasped Sawyer's shoulder.

"Mind if I steal her away?" Upton asked.

Sawyer turned back to his plate, his spine curling forward slightly under Upton's grip. "Go ahead."

"Thanks, mate." He slapped Sawyer once on the back. "Let's go for a walk," he said, offering me his hand now. "It's gorgeous out, and I want you all to myself for a little while before you leave."

I took a deep breath and exhaled, blowing out all the stress about Billings and Easton. There was nothing I could do about it now, and I wasn't going to let potentially imaginary drama ruin my last couple of hours with Upton.

"Sounds perfect," I said, taking his hand.

I gave Sawyer a smile as we walked away, but he was looking in the other direction.

GOOD-BYE FOR NOW

I gazed across the aqua-blue ocean, watching the waves as they lapped at the white sand. Upton's arms were wrapped around me from behind, his chin resting on my shoulder. My heart felt heavy and full. I took a deep breath and let it go, just to see if I could lessen its load, but somehow it felt even heavier.

"What are you thinking?" Upton asked quietly.

"I'm thinking that I'm really going to miss you."

He chuckled, sending a pleasant shiver through my chest. "You sound surprised."

I smiled and sighed again. In a way, I *was* surprised. I couldn't believe that, in such a short time, everything about him had become so familiar to me. The warmth of his skin, the roughness of his cheek on the mornings he didn't shave, the crisp scent of his clothing, the sexy lilt of his accent. And I was going to miss every last bit of it. Every last bit of him.

In a little while, we were going to jet off in different directions, for distant corners of the world. And as much as I knew that saying good-bye was going to hurt, I had to wonder . . . did I really want to be tethered to someone? Did I want to go back to Easton as Upton's girlfriend and have to second-guess myself every time I flirted or needed a date for a party or met a guy I really liked? It kind of went against the whole carpe diem lifestyle I'd promised myself I'd have back when I was on the island.

I had to say something. I had to be honest with him. And I had to get it over with before my heart burst.

"Upton, about this whole long-distance thing," I said, turning to face him. He kept his arms around my waist so that our faces were extremely close.

"You're going to get all practical on me now, aren't you?" he asked, giving me a quick kiss.

"It's just . . ." I took a deep breath and fiddled with the buttons on his white linen shirt. "It doesn't seem all that realistic."

"I know," he said.

I glanced up at him, feeling both hopeful and disappointed at the same time. Is it wrong that part of me wanted him to fight me on this? "You do?"

"Well, I can't expect a girl like you to just cloister yourself away, can I?" he said with a smirk. He tucked my hair behind my ear, then ran his hand down the length of it.

"It's not that I don't care about you . . . I mean, I do," I said in a rush. "It's just, I've got this whole new seize-the-day thing going on and—"

"After three near-death experiences and six days trapped on a deserted island by yourself, I supposed that's to be expected," he said with a shrug.

I laughed. "So you understand?"

"Of course," he replied. "But does this mean it's over and done? No more Reed at all? I've got to quit you full stop? No calls or texts or anything? Because I don't think I'm ready for that."

My smile brightened. "I don't think we have to be that drastic," I said, pulling him closer. "What if we say we'll stay in touch and just . . . see what happens?"

"And maybe see each other over spring break? I mean, if neither of us is with anyone else," he clarified quickly. "Because my parents have this villa in southern Italy that you would just adore."

"Southern Italy? I think I could handle that," I said, resting my cheek against his chest. "They don't have deserted islands there, do they?"

"None that I'm aware of. But if they do, I promise to have them populated before March," he joked, holding me tightly.

"I would appreciate that," I replied.

We stood like that for a while, for what seemed like a very long time, until the tide started to come in and the cool water lapped at our feet.

"Reed! They're loading up the car. We've gotta go!" Noelle shouted from the patio outside her house.

"I suppose we should get this over with," Upton said finally.

My heart dropped. "Do we have to?"

He glanced over his shoulder at Noelle, who was giving us a no-nonsense stare from above. "Unless we want to die a slow death at the hands of Noelle Lange," Upton said.

I giggled. "I'll be right there!" I shouted to her.

She rolled her eyes, groaned, and went back inside. Upton smiled down at me, his arms draped around my waist. "So, this is good-bye?"

"Good-bye for now," I clarified.

"All right then." He reached up and cupped one hand around the back of my neck, his thumb caressing the supersensitive skin below my ear. Shiver city. "Good-bye for now, Reed Brennan."

Then he kissed me and kissed me and kissed me, until our feet had sunk into the wet sand, and my lips went from tingling to numb, and I had memorized exactly how perfect I felt in his arms.

THE GREAT AND POWERFUL OZ

I stared out the window as the private jet lifted from the ground, tugging us smoothly into the clear blue sky. The island dropped away beneath me, and I felt the weight of everything that had happened there falling away with it. A new year, a fresh start. That was what Mr. Lange had said. I was definitely down with that.

"Some vacation, huh?" Noelle said, leaning her head back against the leather seat.

We were sitting across from each other, the only passengers on the plane aside from her mother, who was seated near the back with a sleeping mask covering her eyes. Tiffany and Amberly had left earlier that morning, so this time we had the comfy jet all to ourselves.

"It was definitely exciting," I said wryly.

"Putting a positive spin on things," Noelle said with a smile. "I like it."

My iPhone beeped and I lifted it from my lap. Upton had been texting me ever since I left him on the beach that morning, with funny little updates on what he was doing. This one read, simply:

Up and away. U?

I quickly texted back.

Me too.

"God. Who knew Upton could be so clingy?" Noelle joked.

"It's not clingy. It's cute," I replied. The phone beeped again.

Damn. UR getting further away. I can feel it.

My grin widened. I texted back.

Toughen up or its gonna b a long 2 months!

I hit send, then silenced my phone, tucking it back into my bag. When Upton and I had kissed good-bye on the beach, I had told myself that it was our last kiss. That I had to go back to Easton and live my life as if Upton and I had never happened. That was how I had decided it should be. Besides, Upton had always been a player. Whatever we had been through together, no matter how much he swore he wanted to keep in touch, I had to be realistic. I knew there was a good chance he was going to forget all about me the second I walked away.

But apparently that was not the case. And it felt nice.

"So, your parents are meeting you in New York?" Noelle asked.

"And my brother, Scott," I said, a thrill of anticipation running through me at the thought of actually being with my entire family at the same time. I only had one day before I had to be back at Easton for second term—not enough time to go all the way back to Pennsylvania. So my family had decided to drive out to New York, and Mr. Lange had offered to put them up in a hotel for a couple of nights so we could all hang out. I had been hoping they could all meet, considering everything Noelle's dad had done for me on the island, but he was on his way to California for some business meeting. It seemed like no one I knew was ever in the same place with their parents for very long.

"Mmmm. I finally get to meet Scott Brennan," Noelle said, actually licking her top lip.

"Ew. No. I think you two should stay very far away from each other," I said.

"Afraid I'll eat him alive?" Noelle asked with a smirk.

"He'd puddle at your feet," I replied.

"Fair enough." She looked out the window and sighed. "I can't wait to get back to Billings and get you moved into my room. One more term and I finally get that elusive diploma."

For the first time in a long while, I found myself thinking about everything Noelle had been through in the past year. The trial after Thomas's murder, getting expelled from Easton, being on probation. She was supposed to graduate last spring, but that hadn't happened thanks to her punishment. Last fall, however, her father had found a way to get her back into Easton and she'd spent the last few months repeating the first half of her senior year. Now she was actually going to get to finish out her high school career and get on with her life. But she was going to be a year behind all her peers—behind Dash and Natasha Crenshaw and all the others. It must have been torture for a person like her, a girl who was always in charge and in the know, to be bringing up the rear for once.

And now she was so looking forward to getting back to Billings when who knew what surprises might be waiting for us there? I couldn't handle the idea of her not knowing, not being prepared for the fact that Billings might be threatened—again. I took a deep breath and decided to take the plunge.

"Noelle, Sawyer said something to me at brunch this morning about a conversation he overheard between your dad and his dad and someone on the phone."

Noelle lifted her head and eyed me curiously. "About?"

"He said they kept mentioning Billings, and basically, it just sounded bad," I told her, fiddling with the string on my hooded sweatshirt. "I think they might be talking about splitting us up again."

Noelle laughed. "Uh, no. If that were happening, I'd know about it."

"But I—"

"Reed, please," she said, pushing her hair behind her shoulder. "Leave the heavy thinking to me. If there was anything going on with Billings, Daddy would have told me. End of story."

I wanted to believe her. Normally I would. But I couldn't get Sawyer's words out of my mind. *"For the good of the school . . ."*

"But your dad doesn't know everything, does he?" I said, shifting in my seat. "It's not like he's on the board or anything."

Noelle laughed openly, shaking her head as she reached for the *W* magazine on the table in front of her. "No. No board appointment for Daddy. He likes to work behind the scenes. Kind of like the great and powerful Oz."

My brow knit as I looked at her. What did that mean? Did her father somehow have *more* power than the board? I had never even seen him before this trip. As far as I knew, he hadn't been to campus in the year and a half I'd been at Easton.

"But I—"

Suddenly Noelle snapped the just-opened magazine shut and looked up at me, her eyes bright. "I just had the most fabulous idea! You and your mother should join us at Bliss tomorrow!"

Okay. I guess we were changing the subject.

"Noelle, that's really nice, but there's no way we could afford—"

"Shut up. We'll just put it on our tab," Noelle replied. "Come on. You know you need to relax before school starts. And has your mother ever even *had* a massage?"

"Not that I know of," I replied.

"A facial?" she asked.

"Definitely not," I said with a laugh.

"Then you *must* come," Noelle said. "Please?"

"What'll my dad and Scott do?" I asked.

She ducked her chin. "Are you kidding? They're going to be in New York for the first time. I'm sure there's some kind of ball game they could go to or some famous pizza they'll just *have* to eat."

I cracked up laughing. It was like she knew them. "Okay, okay. We're in."

"Good. I'll book it right now."

She pulled her iPhone out of her bag and started to scroll through the address book. I sat back and looked out the window again. There was nothing visible now other than blue sky and the even bluer ocean. Somewhere, miles and miles in front of us, were the U.S. and

Connecticut and Easton Academy. We were on our way home. Tonight I would get to be with my family, and tomorrow my mother and I would spend the day with Noelle and her mom blissing out at Bliss. And the day after that, we'd be back on campus, back in Billings and back to our normal lives.

FRESH START

"Okay, so the first thing we do is go to housing and make sure your transfer goes through," Noelle said, tugging her rolling luggage behind her as we made our way around the circle in front of Bradwell. It was freezing out, and we were both wrapped up in warm wool coats again. It was hard to believe that a few days ago I'd actually been overly warm. "We have to get them to send someone over and move the extra furniture out of the triple and into my room. Then tonight we'll have a little party to welcome you back."

My heart skipped a beat at the thought of being in the same room with all the Billings Girls again. "You're sure they're all okay with this?"

"Are you kidding? They're more than ready to grovel at your feet," Noelle said, pushing her huge sunglasses up on top of her head. "I've already got Rose and London on food and decorations, and I wouldn't be surprised if a few of them had some gifties for you to say they're sorry."

I laughed and rolled my shoulders back as we came around the side of Bradwell. I was trying to ignore the pitter-patter of my heart, the blood racing through my veins. Somewhere on this campus was Josh Hollis. How was I going to feel when I saw him? What was I going to say? What would *he* say? I had to play it cool. I definitely could not mention the fact that he'd gone radio silent for more than two weeks. If I did, I'd sound like a pathetic, pining loser and that was *not* how I wanted to come off.

I was Reed Brennan. I was a Billings Girl again. I had a super-hot European boy pining for me. The rest of the world could kiss my butt.

"I can't wait to see Constance's face when we tell her she doesn't have to be in a triple anymore," I said as Noelle hooked a right around the back of the building and started up the pathway toward Billings. "She is just going to—"

My mouth snapped shut as I walked right into Noelle from behind, tripping over her luggage. I almost fell flat on my face, but managed to stop my forward momentum by grabbing her arm.

"What just happened?" I said with a laugh. But Noelle's face was as white as bleached wood. Her jaw hanging open in a way she never would have approved of if she could have seen it. That was when I heard the beeping. The grinding. And smelled the unmistakable stench of diesel fuel.

My heart in my throat, I followed Noelle's gaze, but nothing could have prepared me for what I saw. Or, more accurately, didn't see.

Billings House was gone.

There was a patch of sky where the tall structure used to be. All that remained standing was about half of the west wall. The wall that was once the outer wall of my room. Two ugly yellow backhoes were clearing away stone and brick and dust and rubble. The rubble that used to be Billings. That used to be my home.

Confounded into silence, I looked at Noelle for an answer. She was shaking from head to toe. She dropped her luggage and took two unsteady steps forward.

"What . . . ? What . . . ?"

For once, Noelle didn't know everything.

It wasn't until that moment that I noticed the other students. Dozens of them, dotting the quad. Everyone was bundled up in their winter coats, surrounded by their boxes and laundry bags and luggage. And everyone was watching. Watching those two vehicles dig and shove and maneuver awkwardly around the destruction zone. Some people were wide-eyed, hands covering their mouths as they looked around in confusion. Others were openly laughing, and a few of those noticed us in our dumbstruck tableau and started to point.

"Noelle," I said, grabbing her arm. "What happened? What's going on?"

My touch seemed to snap her back from whatever bad place she'd spun off to. She yanked her phone out of her purse and pushed down on the touch screen so hard I was surprised it didn't shatter. She brought the phone to her ear and exploded.

"How could you not tell me about this!?" she shouted at, I assumed, her father. "It's gone! Billings is gone! You couldn't *warn* me? How could you let this happen?"

Noelle paced away from me toward the wall of Bradwell, which she kept touching with her free hand as she spouted accusations, as if she was trying to ground herself, trying to make sure this was all real. I knew the feeling. I couldn't stop staring at the trees that used to be behind Billings, but were now visible to the entire quad.

It was gone. My home was gone. Where the hell was I going to go?

"Reed."

His voice sent tingles all down my back even as my heart sank all the way into my toes. I was not prepared for this. Not *now*. How was I supposed to wear a happy, unaffected, cool-Reed face *now*? But there was no putting it off. He was standing right behind me.

I turned around to face Josh Hollis . . . and found him standing there with his hand in Ivy Slade's.

"You're here," he said, obviously confused. "I . . . we heard about what happened. I figured you'd still be . . . recovering. I mean, are you all right?"

His green eyes flicked past my shoulder to the spectacle behind me.

"Of course she is," Ivy said. "This is Reed Brennan we're talking about."

She released Josh and hugged me. Hugged me so tightly I coughed. I managed to lift my arms and hug her back, all the while staring at Josh. He had to give me something here. A mouthed word, a look, a smile—something to let me know what he was thinking. But he simply stared at me. His expression was completely unreadable.

"How are you feeling?" I asked Ivy as I released her. She looked good. She looked, in fact, healthy—like she'd added some weight to her formerly skeletonish frame. There was color in her cheeks, and her dark eyes were bright and happy. Her black hair was back in a tight ponytail, and the pink scarf around her neck was definitely her color.

"I feel amazing," Ivy said. "Nothing like starting over, right?"

The depth of my disappointment was going to suck me down into the frozen earth. My new start had been crushed before I could even begin. I was about to respond. To say something witty, hopefully. Something that would let them know I had been completely aware that Billings was going down and that I was totally fine with it. But then a limousine pulled up on the circle behind them and Sawyer stepped out of the backseat, and suddenly, I didn't want to be talking to them anymore. I didn't want to talk to anyone I had to be fake with or put on an act for. I was too tired. Too over it. Too done.

And Sawyer was right there. He'd gotten his hair cut—not short, but short enough that I could see his eyes—and he looked boyishly handsome in a gray wool coat and black pants. He found me with his eyes and smiled that sweet, vulnerable smile of his, and something inside me responded. Josh must have seen it in my face, because he turned around and gave Sawyer and Graham, who had now joined his brother, a quizzical look.

Behind me there was an awful crumbling sound, followed by a tremendous crash. The students on the quad hooted and cheered and yelped as the last wall of Billings went down. Noelle shouted into her phone. Sawyer lifted his hand in a wave. Josh looked back at me, the curiosity blatant on his face. For a moment I couldn't think of what to do. Where to go, who to turn to, how to begin. So I just closed my eyes. Closed my eyes to all of it and breathed.

My life had just gotten very interesting.

The PRIVATE series
KATE BRIAN

Welcome to Easton Academy, where secrets and lies
are all part of the curriculum . . . but these secrets
must be kept private whatever the cost.

Set in a world of exclusive boarding schools, Kate
Brian's compelling *Private* series combines the bitchy
snobbery of the elite and wealthy, with secrets,
mystery and satire. Dark, sinister and sexy
– with no parents around to spoil the fun . . .

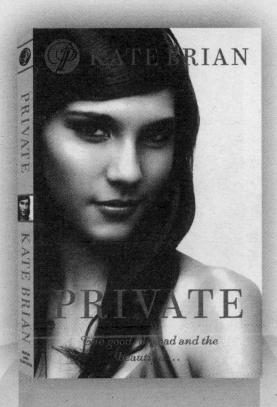

PRIVATE

*The good, the bad and the
beautiful...*

KATE BRIAN

Reed Brennan is delighted when she wins a scholarship to
Easton Academy. But when she arrives at the beautiful,
tradition-steeped campus, everyone is more sophisticated,
more gorgeous and a WHOLE lot wealthier than she is. Reed
may have been accepted to the Academy, but she certainly
hasn't been accepted by her classmates. She feels like she's
on the outside, looking in... until she meets the Billings Girls.

They're the most beautiful, intelligent and powerful girls
on campus. And Reed vows to do whatever it takes to be
accepted into their inner circle. But she discovers much more
than designer clothes hiding in their closets –
there are also plenty of skeletons...

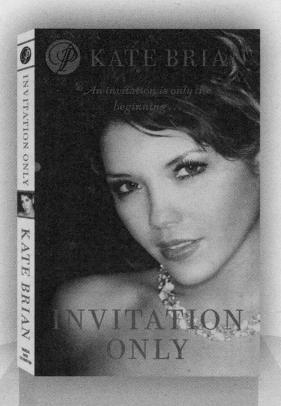

Reed Brennan is living her dream – not only is she a student
at the private boarding school, Easton Academy, she's been
invited to live in the ultra-exclusive Billings Hall, home to the
most beautiful, intelligent and enviable girls on campus.
Life couldn't be more exciting!

But one night of partying in the woods leaves her new
roommate, Natasha, with some very incriminating photos
of Reed on her phone. Suddenly Reed finds herself being
blackmailed against the very girls responsible for
her catapult to campus hot girl – the Billings Girls.
And then there's the nagging fact that Reed's boyfriend,
Thomas Pearson, is missing…

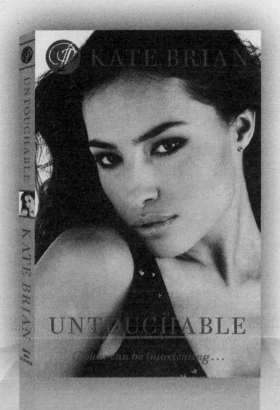

Reed's boyfriend, Thomas, is dead, and life at
Easton Academy suddenly feels very different. Noelle is
being nice, which is totally bizarre; Taylor can't make
it through an hour without bursting into tears; Kiran is
spiking every drink she consumes; and Arianna is acting
as if nothing could be more normal. And then there's Josh.

Left alone on campus for the weekend, Reed and Josh
have to confront their hidden feelings. But when the
Billings Girls return, there's no fun game of tell-all,
instead Josh begins to look like the number one suspect in
Thomas's murder. Surely everyone wants to know
the truth... don't they?

It's a new school year, and Reed Brennan steps back
onto Easton Academy's ivy-covered campus ready to put
the dramatic events of last year behind her. So when the
headmaster forbids Billings Hall from holding their traditional
secretive initiative, Reed is relieved. She champions the
new rules and welcomes the new recruits to Billings Hall.

But there's one Billings resident who's adamant that the
old ways should be kept alive – no matter what,
or who, stands in her way...